LIL MAMA A RYDER

A Chicago Love Story

KEVINA HOPKINS

Cole Hart
SIGNATURE NOVELS

Lil Mama A Ryder: A Chicago Love Story

Copyright © 2020 by Kevina Hopkins

Mailing List

To stay up to date on new releases, plus get information on contests, sneak peeks, and more,

Go To The Website Below...

www.colehartsignature.com

Cole Hart
SIGNATURE NOVELS

THANK YOU

To our loyal Cole Hart Signature readers,

Cole Hart Signature is always growing and changing. Some of you have been following Cole Hart since the beginning of his career, while others have seen us go from Cole Hart Presents to Cole Hart Signature. Then there are our daily new supporters who've only known us for what we are as a company today. Despite our changes, how or when you became a fanatic, we want to kindly thank you for the support.

We appreciate all our Cole Hart Readers because without every single one of you, we wouldn't be the company we are today.

If this book is your first introduction to our company, welcome! And be sure to sign up for email list by click the link, http://bit.ly/2BtGCXH, and joining out text-mail list by texting Cole-HartSig to (855)231-5230. Cole Hart Signature also has a Facebook group where fans get to discuss the plot, characters, overall releases about their favorite book. If itching for new and interesting conversation, click the link, https://geni.us/ColeHartSignatureRead, to join today!

Lastly, Cole Hart Signature is always interested in partnering with aspiring authors, new or experienced, who thrive in the African Urban Fiction and Romance Fiction genre. If you're interested in joining our team, go to www.colehartsignature.com/submissions.

Once again, we truly appreciate all the support over the years.

Much Love,
CHS

INTRODUCTION
PRESENT DAY

Chyna stood looking out of her bay window. The view before her was breathtaking; she was living in her dream house. Her lawn was freshly manicured, and her garden was blooming; to even be able to stand there was a blessing of its own. She had been through hell and back over the past seven years. She endured more than any young woman should have to endure in one lifetime.

Chyna was tested and had to prove herself day in and day out. The game was different for bitches than it was for niggas. They didn't want to hear how a woman started pulling in six figures a month from the streets when they weren't even able to make a quarter of that. The crazy part was, Chyna was willing to teach them the game, but instead of listening, they'd prefer her head on a platter.

Chyna was a hustler and Ryder by nature. The shit ran in her blood, and she learned how to use what she had to get what she wanted. Her goal was to get rich by any means necessary. Even if that meant to get in bed with the devil himself.

"Chyna, are you going to at least talk to me today? We've been doing this for two months now. I come here and sit for however long you want me to, while you just look out of the window. Don't get me wrong, I like free money, but I would love to help you. I know you didn't hire me because you're bored. You have a beautiful family and a business that could be capturing your attention," Dr. Taylor said, looking over the rim of her glasses.

Chyna turned around and looked at the therapist she had hired; it was something that her fiancé had suggested she do. She had been engaged to him for almost two years and still hadn't picked a wedding date. To him, it felt like something was holding her back and before he married her, he had to make sure he had her all. It wasn't that she wanted to waste the therapist's time because hell, she was wasting her time as well. Some things that happened in her past, and she wanted to leave them there. There was so much pain there that she hated thinking about it. There were things done to her that would have broken the strongest soldier, but she took it with stride. However, she knew in order for her to live her best life and truly be happy with someone, she needed to love herself, first, and that started with embracing her past.

"Okay, you're right. The thing is, I don't even know where to begin."

"How about you start from when your life changed the most, and then we'll take it from there," Dr. Taylor suggested.

Chyna laid down on her white sectional and thought about what her therapist suggested. She couldn't believe that she was about to cut open some wounds that had barely even healed, but she knew it was what had to be done if she didn't want to lose the love of her life. He had been very patient, and she felt like she was being selfish to him.

It's now or never. Chyna thought as she twirled the beautiful ring on her finger.

"Okay, that's simple. It all started June of 2013. A week after my eighteenth birthday. Never did I think my life would turn out the way it did. Nothing had gone as I had planned."

THE BEGINNING

C hyna looked down at her phone and saw that it was almost six thirty. She had to hurry up and finish getting dressed because her friend, Brianna, would be there at seven to pick her up. If she wasn't finished in time, she wouldn't hear the end of Bri's complaints. They were going to the Golden Dome to hang out with some friends, so she wanted to make sure that she was looking and smelling good. She rubbed on her Beautiful Day lotion and sprayed on the body spray before putting her clothes on. She decided on a pair of denim skinny jeans that showed off all her natural curves and a white crop top along with a pair of white ones. She finished the outfit off with a silver gold cross and hoop earrings.

Chyna combed her long hair down and applied a light coat of make-up. She was already naturally beautiful, but she wanted to enhance her looks, so that she could look a little older. Once she was satisfied with the outcome, she grabbed her purse and back-pack since she didn't plan on going back home that night.

She walked down the stairs and was stopped in her tracks by the sound of her father's voice.

"Where do you think you're going without saying anything!" her father yelled out.

"My bad, I didn't know you were here," replied Chyna.

"It doesn't matter if I'm here or not. You know you're supposed to let me, or your mother know your whereabouts."

"I already talked to Ma, so she knows that I was going out. I did the chores she wanted me to do around the house."

"Okay, well, just make sure you're back home on time. You know your curfew is at twelve."

"I'm not coming back home, tonight. She said that I could spend the night at Bri's house."

"Yeah, we'll see about that," her father spat as he pulled out his phone.

She knew he wasn't doing anything but calling her mother like he always did. She didn't care how mad he got, she was still going to go outside. She was tired of her father always being so strict with her. She had just turned eighteen last week, and she just knew he would have let the reigns loose a little bit now. She had maintained an A average in high school and was class vale-dictorian. She never gave them any problems, but yet he always found something to trip about.

Chyna waited for five minutes while her father argued on the phone with her mother before he gave the okay for her to leave. She wasted no time running out of the house, just in case he wanted to lecture her about something else. She was glad when she saw Brianna's car out front already.

"Damn girl, it took you long enough," Brianna stated as Chyna climbed into the car.

"Damn, hello to you too, bitch," Chyna said sarcastically to her friend.

"I text you twice and told you that I was outside, so chill with the attitude because I almost left your ass."

"Man, I was down the stairs on time, but then my dad stopped me and started tripping as usual. I swear, I can't wait to get the hell up out of that house."

"I know but look on the bright side of things. You will be

starting college and living in your own apartment in three months."

"Yeah, you're right, but knowing my dad, he'll find a reason for me to stay home," Chyna said as she looked out the window.

Chyna loved her parents to death, but they were always treating her like she was a fragile child. They were never as strict with her big brother or sister the way they were with her. She didn't know if it was because she was the only child left in the house or if her father was just paranoid.

"Aye, snap out of that mood. You came out, so that we can have a good time," Brianna said as she turned the radio up.

Brianna and Chyna had been friends since their freshman year of high school. Their personalities were different, but that's what made their friendship so much better. They had always been there for each other and had secrets that they would take to the grave.

Brianna drove around the dome and parked her car. They grabbed their jackets then walked around until they found their group of friends. All of them spoke, then started drinking and passing a blunt around.

"You know you looking real good right now, Chyna. When you gone stop playing and let me take you out?" Charles asked as he licked his lips.

"How many times do I have to tell you that it's not going to happen? We've been around each other for as long as I can remember, but now that I have an ass and a little meat on my bones, you want me?"

"What can I say? The past year did your body good."

"Yeah, I can't argue with you there," Chyna said with a chuckle.

Up until last year, Chyna didn't have much of a shape. She was five-seven and weighed one hundred and twenty-five pounds with a small ass and thirty-two B breasts. She was tired of feeling like a twelve-year-old and attracting only young boys her age. None of them ever piqued her interest, and it felt like a waste of time going out on dates with them, so she stopped. She wanted to be able to pull the older guys because they were on boss status. She needed a man that was on his grind with money. She came from money and was used to getting whatever she wanted, so she couldn't see herself being with someone that couldn't take care of her. Plus, their swag was on a level of what she was used to being around.

Chyna started eating more, taking vitamins, drinking shakes, and working out. Within six months, she had the body that she desired. She was now one hundred and forty-five pounds with thirty-six C breasts. They still weren't the size she wanted, but a good push-up bra enhanced them more. She was also a size six now and thick in all the right places. She had gotten a body at the age of seventeen, that most grown women desired, and now that she was eighteen, her confidence spoke volumes. She was the definition of a bad bitch, and no one could tell her otherwise.

Eventually, she started getting the attention she wanted from men, even though she hadn't found the right one that was worth settling down with. She just enjoyed flirting and knowing that she could have them if she wanted. Plus, if her father or brother found out she had a thing for grown men, they would kill him and lock her away.

Brianna and Chyna stood and kicked it for almost two hours until Brianna's phone started ringing. A smile instantly spread across her face she walked away from the group. Chyna knew that could only mean that one of her boy toys was hitting her up.

"Aye, Chyna, come here for a minute," Brianna called out.

Chyna walked over to where Brianna was standing. "What's up?"

"You ready to get out of here yet? Tim just called and him and his boy at his house chilling, and they wanted us to come by for a minute."

"Who is his boy? I'm not trying to be stuck there with nobody, I don't know."

"I don't know, but I promise we won't have to stay long. I'm trying to get this money from him, so that I can get the shit I need, and the only way he gone give it to me is if I spend some time with him."

"Okay, fine, but I'm not trying to be there all night."

"We won't, and you might just have a good time."

The girls said their goodbyes and headed towards the car, when someone grabbed Chyna's arm. Chyna turned and looked at the guy, then snatched her arm away. He was a cutie, but she didn't care how fine he was. She didn't like to be touched without permission.

"My bad, lil mama, I didn't mean any harm. I just didn't want you to leave without me getting your attention first."

"Okay, it's cool, what's up?"

"What's your name, beautiful?"

"Chyna, what about you?"

"Everybody calls me Tez. Can I get your number?"

Chyna was about to give him her number until she heard somebody call her name. She turned around and saw that it was her big brother. She cursed under her voice for getting caught out there. She knew he was going to be pissed.

"Yo, Tez, what the fuck you doing in her face?"

"Awe, this you, Rome? My bad," Tez said with his hands in the air surrendering.

"This is my fucking baby sister."

"I swear, if I knew she was your little sister, I wouldn't have approached her."

"Just don't let the shit happen again," Rome snapped.

Tez all but ran away from Chyna and Rome. All she could do was shake her head because she hated how dudes bitched up just from the sound of her brother or the mention of his name. Both her father and brother's names rang volumes in the streets from being over the Black Renaissance Organization. It was a group that her father started from the bottom along with one of his brothers and best friends. They originally started in Chicago and ventured out to Cali as well as Atlanta. The three founders were close to retiring and now the heirs were in the process of taking over. They were known for their organized crime; they dealt with weapons, drug trafficking and money laundering. They had legit businesses as well; there were a couple record labels, beauty shops, and clubs ran by the organization.

"Aye, Rome, you can't blame him though. Lil sis not looking so little anymore," one of Rome's friends stated.

"Man, shut yo ass up. Let me talk to my sister for a minute, then I'll catch up with y'all," Rome said as he pulled Chyna's arm gently, so that they were away from the crowd.

"Why are you always doing that shit? You're so damn embarrassing!" Chyna snapped.

Rome ignored her rant and pulled her into his arms and hugged her tight before letting go. "I don't care how embarrassing you think it is, I'll always look out for you. You don't have any business being out here in the first place, then you in a grown ass nigga's face. I can smell the weed and alcohol on you. I know mom and pops don't know where you are. You keep this shit up, you gone end up with a bodyguard."

"Okay, just please don't tell them," pleaded Chyna.

"You know I'm not going to tell on you, but you need to be careful and slow down. You're barely eighteen years old. There's no need to rush it, Chy."

"I'm just having a little fun, Rome. I only flirt a little bit. It's not like I'm having sex with any of them."

"I know, but these men try to talk to you because they want to get in your pants. They don't look at it as innocent flirting. You're a beautiful girl, and men will use that to their advantage."

"I know that, and that's why I've been extra careful."

"Okay, just don't let me catch you out over here again. I'll be by the house tomorrow to drop off some kicks and outfits that I have for you. We're also going to go to the range, so be ready by four and don't tell pops where we're going."

"I know, I'm not crazy," replied Chyna.

Rome always looked out for his little sister. He made sure that she stayed rocking the latest kicks and outfits. He even kept her pockets laced. He wanted to show her the finer things in life, so that no broke nigga could ever impress her.

"Okay, thank you, big brother. I love you."

"You're welcome, and I love you more. Now, get out of here because you know how these niggas start acting crazy."

"I was just about to leave anyway," Chyna replied as she walked to Brianna's car.

Brianna was just pulling off when the sound of gunshots rang out of nowhere. Chyna tried to open the door, but Bri locked it and drove away fast.

"What are you doing? I have to make sure my brother is good."

"What the hell can we do back there? Rome and his boys strapped, so they can take care of themselves. Just give it a few minutes, and he's going to call you."

Chyna sat back in her seat nervously and shook her leg until her phone started to ring. It felt like she had been waiting for an eternity when it was really only three minutes.

"Hey, are you okay!" Chyna yelled into the phone.

"Yeah, I'm good. Make sure you go straight to Bri's house right now."

"We're on our way as you speak," Chyna lied.

"Okay, I have to go handle some business, but make sure you're ready tomorrow when I get there."

"Okay, just be safe."

"Always," Rome replied before hanging up the phone.

"See, I told you, now you can breathe," joked Brianna.

"Whatever," Chyna said as she turned up the radio.

One thing about Chyna was that she didn't play when it came to Rome. She had a big sister too, but she wasn't as close to her as she was to him. Her sister, Chloe, was seven years older than her, and Rome was eight. He treated her more like his daughter than his sister. Even though he got on her nerves at times, they had a very close relationship, and she opened up to him about things that she would never tell her parents.

Deep down inside, she knew her attraction for older men had a lot to do with the game her brother taught her. All of the qualities he told her that she should look for in a man before settling down, did not fit a boy her age.

2

Bri parked in front of Tim's house. Chyna looked in the mirror, then applied a new coat of lip gloss before she got out of the car. Bri rang the doorbell, and Tim opened the door for them. They walked into the living room and saw a tall, dark, and handsome man sitting on the couch playing the game. He was muscular with the complexion of Hershey's chocolate.

"Bri, Chyna, this is my boy, Josh. Josh, this is Bri and her home girl I was telling you about."

"What's up ladies," Josh spoke with a smile.

Chyna felt weak in the knees just from his smile alone. She loved a man with pearly white teeth, and his fine ass had the nerve to have not one but two dimples.

"Hey," Bri and Chyna said in unison.

Chyna sat on the couch next to Josh while Bri sat on Tim's lap in the love seat.

"We have some patron and Henny. Choose your poison," said Tim.

Bri poured a shot of Hennessy while Chyna mixed a cup of vodka and cranberry. She wasn't trying to get drunk because she didn't know them that well. Josh paused the game so that he could give them his attention. They all sat around and drank shots and smoked until Tim and Bri started getting frisky.

"Yo, take that shit in the room. I'm not trying to see y'all fuck!" barked Josh.

Chyna couldn't do nothing but laugh at how outspoken he was.

"He's right, baby, maybe we should take this to the bedroom," suggested Tim.

"Are you cool with being out here for a little while?" Bri asked Chyna.

Chyna could tell that Brianna was hoping that she said yes. She was about to reply, but Josh answered for her.

"Y'all go take care of y'all business. Shorty will be alright out here with me. I'm not a rapist or no so shit like that."

Bri looked and Chyna and waited for her to give the okay. No matter how bad Bri wanted some dick, she wouldn't leave Chyna by herself if she wasn't comfortable.

"It's cool. I'll be alright, you know I can handle myself," Chyna said with a smirk.

That was all Tim needed to hear. He lifted Bri from his lap and led her to one of his bedrooms in the back.

Once Tim and Bri were out of the room, Josh turned to face Chyna, so he could give her his full attention.

"You're beautiful as hell, but you look young. How old are you?"

"I just made eighteen last week."

"Damn, you're ass still a baby. I'm almost twenty-four."

"Eighteen is legal though," Chyna said with a smile.

"I don't know, shorty. That's still barely legal."

"Okay, how about we exchange numbers, and then when you comfortable about the idea, you can hit me up."

Josh pondered the idea for a minute before picking up his phone, so he could exchange numbers with her. Josh would have never fuck with somebody as young as Chyna, but he couldn't deny how beautiful she was. Not only did she have a cute face, but her body was banging as well. He could definitely see himself having some fun with her.

They continued to talk a little longer, then played NBA live until Tim and Bri came out of the room. Chyna suggested they head to Bri's house before she got too drunk to drive home. Once they made it to the house, they both took hot showers and called it a night.

The following morning, Chyna woke up around eleven and smoked with Bri before heading home around noon. When she walked into the house, she found her parents sitting on the couch watching TV.

"Hey," Chyna spoke as she headed towards the stairs.

"Hey, how did you get home?" Chyna's mother asked.

"Bri's mother dropped me off on her way out."

"Well, your father and I were talking, and we decided that you should hold off on getting an apartment. We can revisit the idea after your second year of college."

"So, how am I supposed to get to school? It's not like there's a bus route to there from here."

Your father and I will alternate our schedules, so that we can take you to school and pick you up, or we can get one of the guys to take you back and forth if you prefer that."

"What? No, this is some straight bullshit. That's not what we agreed on."

"Watch your damn mouth, don't you ever speak to your mother like that again!" Chyna's father yelled.

"I don't mean any disrespect, dad, but this isn't fair. This is not what we agreed on when I started doing my college applications. Just because Chloe stayed here until she was twenty-one doesn't mean I want to, and you let Rome move out when he was eighteen."

"We didn't say that you had to wait until twenty-one. We just feel you're not ready to be on your own yet. You could have gone to one of the schools close to here like your sister did and started helping with one of the businesses.

"I'm sorry that I'm not like Chloe. I don't want to get by just because I'm your daughter. It shouldn't matter what school I choose though. I got the grades that I needed to go to any school that I wanted to. It's not like y'all paying for the school. If I had my way, I would have gone to school in New York, but I agreed to stay in Illinois because you didn't want me to go far away. In return, you said you'd paid for my apartment. The school is only forty minutes away. I worked my ass off, so that I could keep my end of the deal. I maintained a 3.8 GPA throughout high school when I could have been on some dumb shit wilding out, but instead, I was here busting my ass most night. Had I known y'all weren't going to get my apartment, I could have applied for student housing."

"Everything doesn't always go as we plan, Chyna. There's a thing called changing your mind, and that's what we did. Right now, is just not the time for you to be on your own. We can revisit this conversation next year when you're a little more mature," said Chyna's father.

"Whatever, I swear, I hate this fucking house," Chyna fumed as she ran up the stairs to her bedroom and slammed the door shut. Tears instantly fell from her eyes.

Chyna climbed into her bed and powered her phone off. It didn't even surprise her that they had found another way to try and control her. There was no way in hell she was going to have her parents picking her up and dropping her off. Neither was she going to have one of her father's men driving her around. She didn't care what she had to do; she wasn't going to let them ruin her plans. She knew they suggested that, so that she would back down and go to a college closer to them, but it wasn't going to happen unless it was on her own terms.

An hour had passed when there was banging on Chyna's bedroom door. She climbed from the bed and went to open the door and found her sister standing there.

"What do you want, Chloe?" Chyna asked, taking a step back.

"I came to visit y'all, and mommy told me you were having another one of your tantrums. When are you going to grow up and realize that everyone in this family has to make sacrifices? Do you think I was able to do everything I wanted growing up? I had a different career path in mind and all. Only Rome was granted that luxury to do as he pleased since he was a guy."

"I'm really not trying to hear this damn speech again. I'm all for making sacrifices for the family. That shouldn't mean I have to be controlled though. I do every fucking thing they ask of me with no questions asked, but this isn't something I'm just willing to budge on."

"Look, I know it's frustrating, Chyna, but you have to just know when to shut up and listen. Maybe, dad has a reason for why he doesn't want you away but just hasn't told you for your own safety."

"Fuck that, if that's the reason then he should tell me that and maybe I'd be more understanding. Because right now, their reason sounds like bullshit, so I'm going to call them out on it."

"It doesn't matter what their reason is. You still need to be respectful and fix your attitude."

"Okay, this conversation isn't going anywhere. I don't feel like talking anymore. Can you please get out of my room?"

"I don't have to go anywhere. You don't pay not one bill in this house."

"I said get out of my room!" Chyna yelled as she lunged and pushed her sister backwards.

Chyna and Chloe began to tussle until her father ran up to the room and broke them up.

"What is going on up here with you two? I didn't raise y'all to behave like this."

"That's her, she just attacked me out of nowhere!" Chloe screamed.

"Oh, cry me a fucking river. I asked you to get out of my room nicely, and you didn't listen."

"Chyna, if you keep this behavior up, you're going to be grounded."

"Grounded? Did any of you all forget that I'm eighteen and out of high school now?"

"I don't care how old you are. As long as you're under this roof and have the word teen at the ending of your age, you're to abide by my rules."

"Whatever; do what you want like you always do. Just get your daughter out of my room, now."

"Since you seem to can't comprehend what I'm saying, you'll have two weeks to think about it."

Chyna huffed and puffed then balled her fist up and punched a hole in the wall, causing blood to drip from her knuckles.

"You're bleeding, let me see your hand," Chloe said, stepping near Chyna, causing her to step backwards. When Chyna's temper flared like that it was best to leave her alone.

"I don't need your help. Please, just leave me alone," Chyna begged as she un-balled her fist.

Mr. Black looked into his daughter's eyes. It was a look that he was all too familiar with. As much as he hated to admit; she had the same exact temper as him, so he knew it was best to leave her alone. He knew that Chyna wasn't crazy enough to raise a hand at him, but that didn't mean she wouldn't try to hit her sister because it wouldn't be the first time.

"Come on, Chloe, let's leave her by herself," he stated as he pulled his daughter along with him.

Chyna slammed the door shut and cried as she sat on the floor. She hated that she was an angry crier. Whenever she was upset, she would cry in hopes that it would help her calm down. She bent over and stuck her head between her knees and took deep breaths. She stayed that way until there was another knock at her door.

"Can y'all please get the hint and just leave me alone!" Chyna yelled.

"It's me Chyna, let me in," Rome requested.

Chyna got up from the floor and opened the door then jumped into her brother's arms and began to cry again.

He hugged her tight and allowed her to get all out. "Stop crying, baby girl, and tell me what's wrong."

"I don't want to be here, Rome. They act like I'm burden to them just because I'm not the good little daughter like Chloe."

"That's not true, Chy, you're not a burden to anyone."

"You don't understand how I be feeling. Sometimes, I think that maybe if I just end my life everyone would be much better."

"Look at me, I don't ever want to hear you say no shit like that again, Chyna. Even if you think none of them love you, just remember that I do. Do you think I want to live in a world that my little sister is no longer in? Pack a bag, so that you can come home with me for a little while."

"I'm grounded, so they're not going to let me go."

"Just pack the bag, and I'll take care of the rest."

Chyna took a clean scarf from her drawer and wrapped it around her hand then grabbed some clothes and everything that she needed for school and packed it in a bag. Once she had everything, she headed down to the living room where everyone was at. She could hear her siblings arguing with each other.

"See, that's what her problem is now, Rome. You're always babying her, so now she's a spoiled brat. She needs to be going to see a psychiatrist and being evaluated.

"That's my baby sister, and I won't apologize for looking out for her. I look out for her the same I did for you when we were young. Things have changed a lot since when we were her age. This generation isn't the same as it was when we were growing up. We all know she's strong minded, but she's also a good kid. It's not her fault that she inherited the men in this family's attitude and not mom's like you. She doesn't need therapy. She just needs someone to listen to her and talk to her, not at her."

"Dad already told her she was grounded. You can't have her thinking it's alright for her to undermine him more than she already does."

Chloe was starting to get on Rome's nerves, so he turned his attention to his father. "Let her come to my house, pops. She can be grounded from there. I'll make sure the only time she leaves the house is if it's with me."

"How long do you plan on her staying with you?"

"For however long y'all say it's okay."

"You get one week to try and fix her attitude, or I'm going to send her to stay with your uncle in Memphis for the summer."

Chyna fumed as she watched her family talk about her like she was some delinquent child. She knew that she probably could have handled things differently, but she was upset because college was the one thing that she had been looking forward to since she started high school.

Rome motioned for Chyna to follow, him so she said goodbye to the rest of her family and left with her brother.

"How bad is your hand hurt? Are you still up for going to the range? I was going to take you to the gym, too but that's out of the question since you done fucked up your knuckles."

"My hand is fine. It's not anything that I can't handle."

Rome drove to one of their training centers and parked the car. Him and Chyna spoke to everyone then went to their usual spot. Chyna loved the feeling of pulling the trigger on a gun. It was exhilarating and instantly calmed her down. After about thirty minutes, they went to the gym to punch the bag.

"Do you want to talk about what has you punching walls?"

"Mom and dad found a way to ruin my life," Chyna replied before explaining everything that happened.

"I understand why you might think that, but you need to learn how to control your temper. I tell you that every time we train."

"I did control my temper. If I hadn't, my fist would have collided with Chloe's nose and not the wall," Chyna replied seriously as she punched the bag continuously.

Once they finished punching the bags, they went to run around the track.

"So, what's got you riled up the most? Is it that you can't move out or is that they want to drive you back and forth to class?"

"It's all of it, Rome. That was my ticket to independence. I kept my end of the deal, and they reneged. They probably never planned on letting me go anyway. Had I known this, I could have come up with a backup, and now it's too late for me to even apply for school housing."

"What if I talk pops into letting you move in with me and give you one of my cars to get around in?"

"I don't know, you know it's not that simple."

"Just think about it, even if you don't move in with me, still get one of my cars so that you can get around, and we'll figure out the rest later."

"Alright, I'll think about it."

Rome and Chyna finished up at the gym than grabbed some pizza and chilled until he had to leave out to take care of some business.

3

Two weeks had passed since everything had happened, and Chyna was finally off punishment. Rome stayed true to his word and made sure to pick her up and drop her off every day. She still hadn't decided on rather she wanted to move in with her brother or not. He was just as protective as her father was in a sense, but she was definitely going to take him up on the car offer. Rather she stayed at home or with her brother; it would only be a temporary solution. She just needed to figure what to do so that she could get out on her own. She didn't want to have to depend on anyone.

"Why aren't you dressed yet? What are you wearing?" Bri asked as she walked into Chyna's room.

"Girl, I don't know yet," replied Chyna.

Chyna had been rummaging through her closet, trying to find something to wear to go hang out with Josh. They had been texting each other, and he had been trying to get her to come see him, but since she was in trouble, she made up an excuse not to go see him. Now that she was off punishment, she decided to go.

"Wear something sexy since you're finally going to pop your cherry."

"I'm not popping no cherry, which is why it's hard for me to find something to wear. He's cool and all, but I'm not ready to give up the goods yet. He's going to have to work for that."

Brianna always teased Chyna about being a virgin because she was probably the only one in her senior class; half of them had been passing each other around since Freshman year. Everyone looked at her like she was stuck up or thought that she felt like she was too good for any of them. She had thought about just doing it with someone to get it over with, but she valued herself more than that. When she decided to have sex, it would be with someone she was actually feeling and not just because she was pressured into it.

"Okay, go cute but sexy then. Put on a nice pair of leggings and a top. Give him the vibe of you can look but don't touch."

"Okay, that I can do," Chyna replied.

Chyna grabbed a pair of black leggings and a red halter half-shirt with a pair of red and black Giuseppe sneakers. She pulled her hair into a ponytail and applied a light coat of make-up. She put on her jewelry than looked at herself in the full mirror and smiled. Her body was banging in the outfit she had on.

"Damn, you make me want to play for the other team," Bri complimented her friend.

Chyna grabbed her purse and walked out of the room with Bri.

"Be home by twelve," said Chyna's mother.

"Alright, mother, "Chyna relied as she walked out of the house with Bri.

Chyna got in the car with Bri and sent Josh a message, letting him know that she was on the way.

"So, are you nervous?" asked Bri.

"Girl, yes. I'm trying to get to know this nigga, not bust it open already."

"Just go with the flow, but don't do nothing you're not comfortable with. Have him drop you off at my house by eleven thirty, so that I can take you back home."

"Okay, thank you. I owe you big time for this."

"Don't sweat it. As much as you cover for me, it's the least I can do."

Chyna climbed out of the car and rang Josh's doorbell. It only took about a minute for him to come answer the door. He looked sexy as hell in a pair of black jogging pants and a white tank top.

"Hey, beautiful, come in," Josh said, stepping to the side and allowing Chyna to enter.

"Hey," Chyna replied as she walked into the house.

"Come on, I can give you a tour while we wait on the dinner to arrive." Josh offered Chyna his hand and showed her his house. He had a beautiful three-bed, two-bath upstairs and downstairs home. He even had a finished basement.

"This is nice, Josh," complimented Chyna.

"Thanks, ma, the food is arriving now."

Josh met the Uber Eats driver at the door and grabbed the Longhorn takeout. He would have taken her out to dinner some-where, but she wasn't ready to be in public with him yet.

"I can set the table for you," Chyna said as she grabbed some dishes from the cabinet and placed them on the table.

Chyna transferred the food from the containers and placed them onto the plates for them and poured them something to drink into a cup.

"I know this isn't what you would look forward to for a first date, and I swear, I'm not some cheap nigga but given the situa-tion that we're in, I hope this is fine with you."

"I don't think that you're cheap, and this is perfect. I'm the one that asked if we could stay in today."

"I know, but just know when you ready to go out, I'm going to make sure it's a great date."

"I'll be looking forward to it," smiled Chyna.

Chyna and Josh made small talk over dinner then she cleaned the dishes while he rolled up a couple of blunts and grabbed a bottle from the liquor cabinet. Once Chyna was done, she joined Josh on the couch.

"Man, you sexy as hell, Chyna. You got me ready to risk it all for you."

"I bet, but we just met each other, so I think it's best to get to know each other first. I'm not asking you to commit to me today nor do I want to rush into anything. We can take things on a day-to-day basis. I'm not stupid. I know you have females you're already fucking, and that's fine with me because we're not in a relationship. I'm not ready to have sex with you yet, so I'm not going to trip. All I ask is that you be respectful and keep it a buck with me."

Josh smiled and nodded his head, letting what Chyna had just said sink in. She was definitely mature for her age, and he liked that.

"Okay, I can deal with that, but when the time is right, I'm going to make you mine. So, whatever nigga you fucking with right now better be ready to get they walking papers," smirked Josh.

"We'll see about that. I don't just play hard to get, I am hard to get. You're going to have to work hard if you want to be able to claim me as yours."

"You talk a good game, ma. I swear, all I need is one night with you, and you'll be talking to the beat of a different drum."

"Game on," Chyna said as she picked up the cup of vodka and cranberry.

"So, what do you plan on doing now that you graduated?"

I'm going to University of Chicago and majoring in business management. I've started on a couple business plans, so I just need to get the ball going."

"Okay, I see you, shorty. You have beauty and brains."

"What's your plans within the next couple of years?" Chyna asked.

"Well, you already know that I hustle. I'm also in the process of trying to open a lounge with Tim, and I help manage a barbershop."

"Alright, so you on your boss shit. I like that. Do you have any kids?"

"No, ma'am. I got one of my exe's pregnant when I was younger, but neither of us could afford the baby and the timing was off, so we agreed that it was best she got an abortion. After that, I vowed to never get another woman pregnant unless I was financially stable enough to raise a baby. I would never want to have to be forced to get rid of another one of my seeds."

"Okay, that's understandable."

Josh and Chyna continued to talk for a little while longer until he turned on Deadpool. They were halfway into the movie when Chyna felt Josh looking at her.

"What's wrong?" asked Chyna.

Josh didn't answer Chyna. Instead, he pulled her onto his lap, so she was straddling him. He sucked on her bottom lip before sticking his tongue in her mouth. Chyna had never had sex before, but she had mastered kissing.

Josh slid his hand up under Chyna's shirt and massaged her breast. He couldn't believe that he was actually sitting on his couch making out. He didn't care that he had just met her. The only thing stopping him from whipping his dick out and piping her down was that he knew, she wasn't ready yet, and he wasn't going to force her.

Josh stood up with Chyna on his lap then sat her down on the couch and reached for the rim of her leggings. She gripped his hand to stop him from pulling her pants down.

"I just want to taste it; I promise I'll keep my clothes on."

When Josh saw that Chyna wasn't protesting, he pulled her pants and underwear down then pulled her to the edge of the couch. He put one of her legs over his shoulder and kissed her inner thighs, causing her to arch her back before he even made his way to her honey pot.

Josh smirked before blowing on her clit and placing his lips on it. Her back arched again, and she tried to push him away, but he gripped her thigh tighter. He could tell from that move that she wasn't that experienced.

"Relax, ma. I promise, it'll feel good," Josh assured Chyna.

Josh took his time tongue kissing Chyna's honey pot. The feeling was foreign but very much welcomed.

"Ohhhh, my Goddd, what are you doing to me," Chyna moaned as Josh picked up the pace.

He grabbed her hand and put it on the back of his head. It didn't take no time for her to guide his head to the rhythm that felt good to her. Before she knew what was happening, a feeling of euphoria rushed through her body, and she began to shake.

"Damn, you taste good, ma," Josh said as he stood from the floor.

He kissed Chyna on her lips then went to the bathroom to brush his teeth and wash his face. He grabbed another wet towel and took it to Chyna. She was still sitting in the same exact spot that he had left her in.

"I can't move," Chyna said, trying to stand up.

"Girl, that was me being nice. You haven't seen what I can really do to you. I got to give it to you little by little until you ready for all of me."

Chyna stood from the couch and took the towel from Josh and wiped herself then went to the bathroom to clean up more properly. By the time she made it to the front room, Josh was sitting on the couch firing up a blunt.

Chyna sat down next to him and smoked while they finished watching the movie. By the time the movie was over, it was time for Chyna to leave.

Josh drove Chyna to the block up the street from Bri's house, and they waited while she came to meet them.

"Thank you for tonight. I enjoyed myself," said Chyna.

"You're welcome. I enjoyed myself as well. Make sure to text and let me know when you make it home."

"Okay, I will," Chyna replied before leaning over to kiss Josh on the cheek then getting out of the car.

Chyna got in Bri's car and they drove towards her house.

"Bitch, I know you gone tell me what happened!" exclaimed Bri.

"Well, he ordered take out from Longhorn and we smoked and drank. We tried to watch a movie but ended up making out. Making out led to him giving me head, and then we smoked some more before he dropped me off to you."

"Wait, rewind. The nigga gave you head, and you didn't do nothing for him?"

"Nah, he knows I'm not ready for that yet. I guess, it's his way of making me have something to look forward to when we do have sex, but that's not happening until I'm eighteen. We both agreed on that. I look it at it as waiting until I'm legal and time to get to know each other."

"Well, I'm happy you're finally opening up to somebody. Hit my line tomorrow if you decide to come out with me."

"I can't, I have some family shit to do, and I won't be in town until Monday, so I'll hit you then."

"Okay, I'll talk to you later."

Chyna got out of the car and headed straight up to her bedroom. She grabbed some night clothes and took a shower and climbed into her bed.

4

J osh looked down at his phone and was in the process of
texting Chyna to check up on her. He hadn't heard from
her since she texted him the night before, letting him know
that she had made it home. He knew that she was going away for
the weekend with her family, so he wanted to know how things
were going. She had told him about some of the issues that she
had with her parents and sister, so he wanted to make sure she
was good. Surprisingly, he was genuinely concerned.

"Nigga, are you going to take your turn or what?" DJ asked.

"Awe, my bad," replied Josh.

"The nigga too busy caking," laughed Tim.

"Don't worry about what I'm doing over here," Josh said as
he took his shot.

Tim and DJ had stopped by to discuss some business and
ended up staying around to smoke and play pool. That was the
thing that Josh loved about his house; he could have a good time
without even leaving. He had a mini arcade in his basement.

"So, what's up with you and Chyna?" asked Tim.

"Shit, we just getting to know each other," said Josh.

"Man, don't even waste your time with her. That bitch is
stuck up and high maintenance," spat DJ.

DJ's comment had piqued Josh's attention, so he decided to feed into the statement.

"What makes you say that?" questioned Josh.

"I tried talking to her, and she was all quiet and shit. Hell, we was all at the mall when I met her, and I even offered to buy her some sneakers from Foot Locker, and she declined. Like what bitch you know gone turn down a pair of free shoes?" inquired DJ.

"Nigga, your ass is damn near thirty. That's probably why she was ignoring you. Her ass barely eighteen and have you seen the type of shoes that she rock? She's not going to be impressed by gym shoes from Foot Locker when she's wearing Giuseppe's and LV."

"Man, I'm not about to spend that kind of money on no bitch. I don't care how fine she is."

"Yeah, that's why your cheap ass don't be having no bitches now," laughed Tim.

"Don't even get me started on your tricking ass, Tim. That bitch, Bri, calls you and you giving her whatever she want. I guess, it's a good thing she's not on her homegirl level."

The guys hung out for about another hour before Tim and DJ left to go their separate ways. Josh went up to the master bathroom and took a hot shower then got dressed in a pair of blue jeans and a white V-neck shirt with a pair of Ones. He needed to go pick up some money and do a drop off in Rockford. It was already a little after eight, so he hoped everybody had their money straight, so that it wouldn't take all night because he had a two-hour drive ahead of him.

Josh grabbed his piece from the safe and his jacket then headed to his black Range Rover. It was the car he used when he needed to make runs and collect money because he had hidden compartments to stash his guns, money, and drugs.

His first stop was to his trap house on Grenshaw. The workers on that block sold weed and pills for him; it was mainly young niggas that worked for him over there. He chopped it up with them for a minute and then went over on Laramie to his other block, where the guys sold rocks and blows. He collected the money from them, then cut and bagged the rocks that he needed to drop off at another spot. By the time he was finished with that, it was almost ten, and he had one more spot to hit up.

Josh took the ten-minute drive to the Village Row Houses. He sent Iesha a text, letting her know that he was outside. About five minutes later, he saw her walking to his car with a pair of booty shorts and a tank top while carrying two back-packs. Her red weave was flowing down to her ass. She was a beautiful girl; she was five six and weighed about one hundred and seventy pounds. She had a big ass and thirty-eight DD breasts.

"Hey, baby," spoke Iesha.

"What's up ma. You separated everything, right?"

"Of course, daddy," replied Iesha.

"Alright, cool. I need to drop something off at the house then we can hit the road," said Josh.

Iesha was the ex that Josh had told Chyna about. They had been together off and on for the past six years. They'd never let their personal relationship interfere with their business relation-ship. Since she lived in the Village, she had connections with the weed heads as well as the crackheads. She was able to get a few young boys to run the drugs for her. She bagged and weighed the drugs then distributed it. When she collected the money, she would take her twenty percent of what was made and gave the rest to Josh. He had never had an instance when she was short or played with his money. Even if she was mad at him, she made sure to still take care of business because that was her revenue and way of eating.

Josh pulled up to his house and grabbed the duffel bag, then went in the house and put the bag in the safe. It contained the money he collected as well as a couple pounds of weed. Josh grabbed his overnight bag and then was gone out of the house as quickly as he had entered.

The ride to Rockford was smooth. The first stop was to check into the Hilton Hotel. Once Josh got the room key, he headed up to their room. Josh took all the product from the bags then recounted and weighed it to make sure everything was good. After he was satisfied with that, he hit up his boy, Lamar, to find out when his girl was ready to meet up with Iesha at the gas station.

Whenever Josh went away for deliveries, he always took Iesha with him and had her do the drop off, so that it wouldn't look suspicious.

"Lamar said Drea should be there in ten minutes. Make sure to pay attention to your surroundings at all times. If something feels off, just come back here," said Josh.

"I know, baby, we've been doing this for years now. Plus, I have Ms. Pearly with me, so I'm good."

"Okay, just making sure," replied Josh.

Iesha picked up the keys and the package from the desk and headed out, leaving Josh in the room alone. Josh used that time to roll up a Backwood and call Chyna.

"Hey," Chyna spoke into the phone on the third ring.

"Hey, baby girl, what you up to?"

"Nothing, just laying here in bed."

"You thinking about how good I made you feel yesterday?"

"Yes, I wouldn't mind you doing it again."

"You taste good as fuck, so I wouldn't mind doing it again. I can't wait to be able to make you feel other things though. I'm going to break your little ass in."

"Yeah, we'll see about that."

"So, what you wearing?" Josh asked just as Iesha came through the hotel room.

"Well, since I'm about to go to sleep I'm not wearing anything. I don't like to sleep with clothes on."

"Damn, I can't wait to see you like that. You got my dick

hard as hell right now," Josh replied, not caring that Iesha was standing there and could hear his conversation.

Josh watched as Iesha stormed into the bathroom with a slight attitude. He shrugged his shoulder and continued his conversation with Chyna.

"Down, boy. We still ain't there yet."

"I know we're not, I'm just stating the facts," chuckled Josh.

Josh and Chyna talked for another ten minutes before ending their phone call. He connected his phone to the charger when Iesha walked out of the bathroom with a towel wrapped around her.

"So, you got a new bitch now?"

"Why the fuck is you questioning me, and why do you have an attitude? It's not like you're my girl, Iesha. We both agreed that we were allowed to do our own thing."

"Yeah, but I haven't been fucking with anybody else, Josh. You've been taking me out, and we've been sleeping with each other on the regular. Why do you have to start fucking with somebody else? We've been doing good all this time. Why can't we just get back together? I do everything that you ask and need of me. What more do you need from another bitch?" Iesha asked on the verge of tears.

Josh hated seeing Iesha cry, so he climbed out of the bed and pulled her into his arms.

"I haven't fucked anybody else, Esh. I just be talking and flirting with shorty on the phone. There's nothing going on between me and her, so just calm down."

"I still love you, Josh, and it's time for us to give each other another real chance. It's time for you to forgive and trust me again. We're supposed to start building our family next year. Don't you still want those things with me?" Iesha asked as she caressed Josh's handsome face.

"Look, Esh, I still love you and that will never change. I didn't forget what we planned, but a lot has changed since then. Let's just take things slow and work our way back to that point. I'm willing to try, but your ass can't start acting all crazy again."

"I won't, I promise!" squealed Iesha.

Josh would always have a weak spot for Iesha; they had first started dating when they were seventeen years old. When they met, they both were in a rough place. Josh had been struggling to find a way to come up with some money to get some new shoes and clothes for school. His grandmother was getting social security checks, but they weren't doing shit because not only was she taking care of Josh, she had custody of three of her other grandkids as well. He was raised by his grandmother because his mother was a prostitute and on drugs. She had fucked so many men before she got pregnant, and she had no idea who the father was.

Iesha, on the other hand, was raised in a two-parent home until her father was killed in a hit and run when she was fifteen. Once that happened, her life changed drastically. Her mother couldn't afford to pay the rent, so they were forced to move to the projects. Her mother had fallen into depression and found comfort in the bottom of the bottle. Iesha had two younger siblings, so she was forced to take care of them, so that CPS wouldn't find out what was going on. She had to come up with money to buy clothes and food for the house.

Josh had started selling nickel and dime bags while Iesha had found a job at McDonald's. Neither one of the them were happy about the amount of money they were making, but they had to do what was needed to be done for their family.

They had been together for almost two years when Iesha got pregnant. It hurt both of them to get rid of the baby, but at the time, they didn't see another solution. Neither one of them were in a position to be able to take care of a baby because they could barely take care of themselves. Plus, there was nowhere for the baby to go. Josh was living in a two-bedroom apartment with four other people, and Iesha was living in a three-bedroom apartment that had people coming in and out at all type of hours.

That was not the type of environment that they wanted to raise a child in. Having to make his girl get rid of his baby because he was broke, did something to Josh. He didn't care that he was only nineteen. To him, he was still a man and should have been able do better.

Josh and Iesha never wanted to be put in that situation again and didn't want to have any more slip-ups, so she got on the Mirena which would last five years. They made a plan that within those five years, they were going to get their paper and do what they needed to do, so that when she went to get her Mirena taken out, they could have another baby. By then, she'd be twenty-five and her two siblings would be old enough to move out of their mother's house and take care of themselves.

Josh's and Iesha's relationship was going good for about a year and a half after that. Iesha was still working at McDonald's, and Josh was still hustling, but he had had upgraded from nickel and dimes. His cousin had linked him up with Tim, and he started pushing weight. He was seeing more money than he had ever seen in his life. By the time he was twenty, he had moved into his own apartment and bought his grandmother a house. He was waiting to buy his house because he wanted to flip more money and get a house with Iesha when the time was right.

However,, the more money he got, the problems came with it. He had work nonstop to be at a certain caliber. Iesha automatically thought that he was fucking around on her, and she started acting crazy. She was calling him all day every day and was even popping up at his house, trying to see if she'd catch him with someone else. he didn't like that clingy shit and wasn't going to deal with it. She eventually told him that she had been sleeping with somebody else, and she felt bad, so she wanted to find an excuse for fucking up. The funny thing about it was, Josh didn't even get upset about it because he knew it was her loss. He had been turning women down left and right because he wanted to stay true to the woman that was there when he didn't have nothing, but she was the one to ruin that, not him.

Josh broke up with Iesha and started doing him. He moved out of his apartment and bought the house that he now lived in. In the process, he wanted to make sure that she was straight, so that's when he came up with the idea of her being in control of his work in the projects. Eventually, they started sleeping together, but they were never serious again.

Josh pulled Iesha's towel off of her and stripped himself of his clothes before lying back on the bed. She wasted no time taking his thick dick into her mouth. He closed his eyes and gripped the back of her head while enjoying the pleasure.

"Shit, ma, just like that, fuck," Josh moaned.

Iesha had been fucking Josh long enough to know when he was about to come, and she refused to let that happen before she got hers off. She took her time sliding down his pole. A gasp escaped both their mouths. Josh loved the way Iesha felt, and she knew the way he liked to be fucked. He held onto her breast while she bounced up and down until she was coming. Once she came, he flipped her over onto her back and fucked her hard for about twenty minutes until they both were coming.

Josh laid back on the bed and looked at the time. It was almost three in the morning, and he was tired as hell. He had been up since eight a.m. the following morning. He had busted his nut, so he was ready to K.O. He was falling asleep within five minutes.

"Josh?"

"What, Iesha?"

"Are you sleep?"

"Yes, now what do you want?"

"So, when are you going to tell ole girl that you was on the phone with that you're not interested anymore?"

"Iesha, I'm too fucking tired for this shit right now. Go your ass to sleep. You worrying about the wrong thing," Josh fumed as he turned on his side and closed his eyes.

He couldn't bring himself lie to her in her face, and he couldn't give her a timeframe. He had no intention to stop pursuing Chyna. That was the reason why he didn't agree to get back with her yet. Curiosity got the best of him, and he needed to be able to hit Chyna at least one time. In his eyes, as long as he wasn't in a relationship with either woman, he wasn't cheating.

$\text{\textsection} \quad 5 \quad \text{\textsection}$

Chyna slipped her long sleeve, black Herve Leger mini dress over her head and slid her feet into her three-inch YSL sandal heels. She put her gold anklet on along with her gold chain, bracelet, and earrings. She was just about to put her make-up on when there was a knock at her door.

"Who is it!" yelled Chyna.

"Me, can I come in?" Rome asked.

"Yeah, it's opened," replied Chyna.

Chyna picked up her foundation and started applying it when Rome walked over to her.

"Are you almost done?"

"Yes, you all said seven. I still have fifteen minutes."

"I don't need to tell you to make sure you behave, do I?"

"No, Rome, I won't embarrass you or dad," Chyna said as she finished applying her foundation.

"You don't you don't need all that shit. You're already beautiful," complimented Rome.

"I know, but I like wearing it. I'm only putting a little on."

"Okay, I'll go back downstairs, everyone is already in the living room ready to go."

"Okay, I'll be down in about five minutes."

Chyna finished applying the last of her make-up then grabbed her YSL black handbag and exited the room. She headed down the stairs to where her parents, brother, sister and brother-in-law, Nathan, were waiting.

"What are you wearing, Chyna?" questioned Mr. Black.

"Can we please not start this? This is the only dressed that I packed. So, unless you want me at the dinner party with jeans and a half-shirt on, I have nothing else to wear."

"You couldn't find anything more appropriate?"

"I don't see anything wrong with my dress. My breast not out, and my butt is covered. I could have done way worse than what I have on now."

"It's fine, pops, she's with us and other people from the organization. She's good, and I'll make sure to keep an eye on her," said Rome.

Chyna rolled her eyes at her brother and walked out of the house to his rental. She didn't want to be stuck in the car with her parents, sister, and brother-in-law.

They had flown to Atlanta yesterday morning, so that they could attend the organization's annual picnic and dinner. They alternated between ATL, LA, and Chicago every year. Chyna opted out of going to the picnic and helped her mother get everything together for the dinner. She didn't feel like being around everyone at the picnic because she didn't really talk to any of the other people. Plus, her cousins didn't make to town until this morning, so she would have been stuck by herself. She couldn't get out of going to the dinner even if she wanted to.

"Can I drive?" Chyna asked.

"Yeah," Rome said as he got in the passenger seat.

Chyna climbed in the driver's side of the white Lambo and adjusted the mirrors and the seat before pulling out of the parking spot. She hopped on the expressway and floored the car while Rome sat back in his seat and lit up his blunt. He wasn't concerned about Chyna's driving because he was the one that taught her to drive. He took a few puffs then handed the blunt to Chyna. He didn't like the fact that she smoked weed, but he knew that he couldn't stop her from doing it. He would rather her smoke his shit than to for her to get ahold of some shit that somebody laced. She knew the number one rule to smoking was don't smoke shit that she didn't see get rolled.

Chyna drove for about twenty minutes until they pulled up to the mansion. They had booked a huge mansion for the gathering because everyone was more comfortable that way. None of them wanted to get caught slipping in public with their families. Especially, the ones that didn't live in Atlanta.

Chyna looked in the mirror and applied a new coat of lip gloss then sprayed some of her Versace perfume on before climbing out of the car and handing the key to one of the valet drivers.

Chyna and Rome walked into the house and mingled with some of the guest. He wanted to wait for the rest of his family to get there to take their seats. Being that Chyna was driving like a bat out of hell, it took them about an additional seven minutes to get there.

"Are you ready to sit down or what?" Chyna asked, irritatingly.

"Yeah, we're ready," replied Mrs. Black.

"Chyna, you need to stop driving like that before your license get revoked before you're able to enjoy it," Chloe said in a chastising way.

Chyna opened her mouth but closed it when she saw the pleading look on her brother's face. She wasn't about to embarrass her family in public, so she ignored her sister and walked to the front of the dining area and found the table with their names.

Rome looked at the way the names were set up and switched it around where Chyna was sitting between him and her mother and not her father and Chloe. It was best that he kept her as close to him as he could to keep the peace.

Chyna sat her purse in the seat then walked towards the bar

area where she found her cousins, Joseline and Jerry. They were her father's brother, Jeremiah's, kids. Jeremiah was the brother that ran things out of Cali. Joseline was twenty-two and Jeremiah was twenty-four. Chyna was the youngest person in her family on her father's side. Everyone had grown kids already. She hated being the only young one because she had to sit out a lot of events and stuff because of her age.

"Hey, Chy! Damn girl, I almost didn't recognize you. I see puberty did your body good," laughed Joseline. Joseline hadn't seen Chyna since the last event a year ago. She was a college student, so she didn't show up to a lot of stuff with her father and brother.

"Thanks, cousin, you look good too," replied Chyna.

"What's up, Jerry?"

"Nothing much, you been staying out of trouble?"

"Hmmm, define trouble?" Chyna asked half-jokingly.

"Ignore him, he's been in big brother mode all weekend, and it hasn't worn off yet."

"It's cool, I'm about to go get something to drink, so I'll meet up with you shortly," said Chyna.

Chyna walked over to the bar and ordered a cranberry and vodka. The bartender was nice looking, and she was bored, so she decided to flirt with him while sipping her drink.

"What's your name, beautiful?" the bartender asked.

"Chyna, what's yours?"

"Levon."

"Okay, well, is it alright if I call you Von?"

"Yeah, you can call me whatever you want, beautiful, as long as you call me," flirted Levon.

Chyna tried her best not to laugh at his lame attempt at flirting. That had to have been the corniest thing she'd ever heard. That's why she couldn't talk to regular men because she wasn't attracted to lame shit.

"Aye, there's other people trying to get your attention for a drink," Rome stated, walking up behind me.

"Damn, do you always have to sneak up on me?" Chyna asked as she turned to face her brother.

"What are you doing, Chyna? I thought I asked you to behave."

"I am behaving, I haven't done anything. I'm not allowed to converse with people, now?" Chyna asked innocently.

"You know the innocent act doesn't work on me. What is in the cup you're drinking?"

"Would you believe me if I said cranberry juice?"

"Hurry up and drink whatever's in that cup then get a Sprite and go see what pops want."

Chyna through the vodka back and got the Sprite like her brother said and went with him to find her father. When she found her father, he was standing with Marcel and a few guys. Marcel was the third originator of the Black Renaissance Organization and was over everything that was in Atlanta.

When Chyna and Rome approached the group, everyone crowded.

"You were looking for me, dad?"

"Yeah, come here. I know you remember Uncle Marcel, but these are his boys, Matteo and Maddox. Matteo is eighteen as well, and he's going to Chicago for college."

Chyna looked at her father and waited on him to get to the point, but when he didn't, she turned to face the brothers. Matteo and Maddox were both handsome with brown skin and hazel eyes, but that was the only thing that was similar in the looks department. Matteo was about five-nine and looked like he weighed no more than a buck thirty-five with a pair of glasses on, and his hair was in twists. Maddox, on the other hand, was more of Chyna's speed. He was about six feet and two hundred and fifteen pounds of pure muscles. He had a head full of wavy hair that could make a person seasick and a stance that demanded respect.

"Okay, that's nice. What school are you going to go to?"

"I'm going to go to University of Chicago with you."

"He's going to stay with us in one of the spare bedrooms for a year. I thought it would be a good idea for you two to get to know each other better," said Mr. Black.

"Get to know each other better? What is this some kind of arranged relationship or something? So, this is why I can't move out yet? Did you know about this, Rome?"

"Chyna, now is not the time. We can discuss this in private later," Rome said, looking around and making sure she hadn't caused a scene.

"You know what, fuck it," Chyna chuckled as she stormed away and went to find an area to be alone. She was at the point that she was so mad that all she could do was laugh to keep from crying.

Chyna knew there was a reason her father pulled the stunt about her not moving out, but she just never thought it was that. Some kind of way, Matteo's father must've convinced him to go to school in Chicago and that her father would look out for him. She would have never thought her father would try to pick the man she ended up with. He pulled that shit with Chloe and Nathan, but she didn't think that he was still on that. Nathan was the son of one of Big Rome's workers. He was practically a square, so their fathers figured they were perfect for each other since Chloe was a square too.

Chyna pulled her blunt from her purse and lit it and inhaled the smoke. She wasn't surprised that her father hid the truth from her, but she didn't expect it from Rome to do that. He knew how she felt about the entire situation, and he still didn't say anything. Even when she cried in his arms damn near every night that she stayed at his house. For the first time in her life, her big brother had let her down, and she hated that feeling more than anything.

Chyna welcomed the calmness and peace that came over her until she felt somebody standing in front of her.

"Look, I don't mean any disrespect, but can you please leave me alone?" asked Chyna.

"What, are you seventeen? Does your father know you smoke?"

"I'm eighteen and does it look like I care what my father knows?" Chyna questioned as she took another puff from the blunt then passed it to Maddox."

"They're about to serve dinner," said Maddox.

"I don't care about that either. I don't care about any fucking thing. I just want to disappear from everybody."

"You're too young to be this cynical. You still have a lot of living, baby girl. I'm sure when you're a little older, you'll understand better."

"How old are you?" Chyna asked curiously.

"Why do you want to know? I'm too old to do whatever is going through your head with you," said Maddox.

"I'm glad to see it crossed your mind, but don't flatter yourself. I was just curious."

"I'm twenty-three."

"You moving to Chicago as well?"

"Nah, at least not right now. I'll be there in about a year. One of your uncle's sons want to come down here to Atlanta from Memphis, so I have to train him. Once I finish that, I'm going to go out to Chicago since that's where my brother is, and I'll run shit with your brother because by then, Chicago businesses and stuff would have expanded more.

"Yeah, don't remind me, your brother is sent to ruin my life."

"In his defense, it wasn't his idea. That was the only way my father was going to let him leave Atlanta for school. He's a good kid, you should at least give it a try."

"No offense but look at me and look at your brother. I would have him turned out so fast, your father would wish he never sent him to Chicago. Don't get me wrong, he's handsome and if he got into The University of Chicago, I'm assuming he's smart too, but he's not my type. I'd be too afraid I'm going to break him."

"Awe, so you got jokes, huh," laughed Maddox.

"Nah, I'm just keeping it real. I would never even attempt to date a man that I felt like I could walk all over. Plus, he's too young for my taste."

"I hear you, baby girl, I'm sure it'll all work out for you. Just be careful with the older guys. They'll be the one to break your heart and have you out in these streets looking crazy."

"Maybe, or I'll be that young bitch that they wished they never tried to play with," replied Chyna.

Chyna and Maddox stood outside talking and smoking until the blunt was out.

"Come on, we really have to go in now before the food gets cold. I don't want to leave you out here alone because you might try to jump."

"Oh, look who has jokes now," Chyna replied as she and Maddox walked back into the hall. They each took their seats at the same table. Chyna hadn't looked at the other names on the name tags when they first came in, so she never even realized Marcel and his sons were sitting at the table with them.

"You smell like weed, Chyna," mumbled Rome.

Chyna ignored Rome and picked at the food on the plate in front of her. She didn't even have an appetite, and she hadn't eaten since breakfast early that morning.

Once everyone finished eating, the DJ played music and the guest enjoyed themselves while Chyna got another drink and sat in the corner of the room. A few guys tried to approach her, but she ignored them. It wasn't like she was allowed to talk to any of them anyway because apparently, she was supposed to end up with Matteo.

After sitting around for almost two more hours, the event was coming to an end. A lot of people decided to meet up with each other in a couple hours at one of the clubs. Since Chyna wasn't old enough to go, she was ready to go back to the house they were staying at.

"Remember to keep your head up and everything will work out for you. Why don't you take my number and when you're feeling like the world is against you again, I can help talk you off the ledge?"

"Okay and thanks for the talk," Chyna replied as she saved Maddox's number in her phone."

"No thanks needed."

Chyna left the mansion and headed to her brother's car. She didn't want to be stuck in the car with him, but it was better than the alternative of riding with her parents. She climbed into the passenger seat and put her headphones in then closed her eyes and tried to think about the best approach for everything. She was stressing entirely too much to only be eighteen. She was going to take Maddox's advice though and just let it all go and allow everything else to fall into place.

❦ 6 ❦

Chloe and Nathan had just walked in the house from dinner, and Chloe was still talking about Chyna. He was starting to think she was jealous and obsessed of her younger sister. He couldn't understand why she was going on like that. As far as he knew, Chyna had never done anything bad to Chloe. Hell, there wasn't much Chyna could have done, given the age difference. Chyna was a little girl when Chloe lived under the same roof as her.

"You know I talked to my ma today, and she said that Chyna didn't come home until almost two in the morning? I bet she out here fucking now and don't know how to act."

"Chloe, she's eighteen years old. Y'all have to realize that y'all can't run that girl's life and pick and choose who she's with. If she's out here fucking, your job as a big sister is to make sure she's out here being safe, not bashing her every chance you get."

"Why are you always taking her side? I see the way you be looking at her. You want to fuck her too, don't you?"

"Man, chill out with that bullshit. I don't look at Chyna as nothing more than a sister. I've been with you for the past five years and around y'all way before that. I would never prey on her like that and never cheat on you with your own sister. I take her

43

side because I see things from her point of view. That shit that happened in Atlanta was crazy. The fact that your dad would try to force her to date somebody is crazy."

"Well, it worked out fine between us two and now we're happily married."

"Yeah, but we knew each other first and were friends. She doesn't know them, and he should have at least talked to her about it instead of blindsiding her."

"Whatever, she'll be alright. She's not more special than I was when I was her age. If I couldn't live the life that I wanted, then she shouldn't be able to either."

Nathan listened to what his wife was saying and shook his head. She was one of the nicest people he had ever known. Like she would take the shirt off her back and give it to a stranger, but then acted like she didn't give a fuck about her baby sister.

"Do you hear yourself, right now? Being that you went through the shit, you knew how it felt. Instead of trying to belittle her, you should be trying to look out for her and stand up to your father like your brother does."

"Well, it looks like my brother is in the same boat with Chyna as I am, seeing as she hasn't talked to him since that night in Atlanta, almost a week ago."

"I don't like this side of you, Chloe. You need to get your shit together," Nathan said as he walked into his bedroom.

Nathan looked down at his phone and saw that he had a text from Jade. She was trying to find out if he was ready to come over for the drink, she'd offered him. Jade was a woman that he had met a few weeks ago and one of his boy's parties. Typically, he didn't make a habit out of exchanging numbers with women because he was married. He had never cheated on his wife before, but for the past month, she had been irking his nerves. She was always nagging or complaining about some shit that had nothing to do with her.

Nathan sent Jade a text back, asking for her address and slid his phone back into his pocket.

"I'm sorry, baby, I promise I'll work on doing better. It's just Chyna is a spoiled brat and sometimes, I wish that she'd just grow up, but I'm going to work on being a better sister to her," Chloe said as she wrapped her arms around Nathan.

"Okay, thank you. That's all that I'm asking you. But look, I just got a text from Ryan. He has an emergency, so he wanted me to come in for a couple hours while he takes care of it. Hopefully, Simon can come in early to relieve me, and I won't have to be long."

"Alright, baby, be safe. I'm about to shower and get ready for bed anyway," Chloe said before kissing Nathan on the lips.

Nathan grabbed his keys off the dresser and headed out of the house to his white BMW. He looked down at his phone and saw that Jade had texted her address. She only lived about twenty minutes away from him. He put the address in his GPS and drove to her house. He parked the car in front of the house and sat there for a few minutes, contemplating was he really about to entertain another woman. He looked down at his wedding band and stuck it in the cup holder as if that was going to ease his mind some.

Nathan walked up the couple of stairs and rang the doorbell. About a minute passed before Jade opened the door in nothing but a black thong and bra. Nathan's dick immediately jumped at the sight of her. She had the most amazing body that he had ever seen. From the looks of it, he could tell that she'd bought her body, but he didn't care. She had smooth dark skin and looked like she had to be about five six and weighed no more than one hundred and forty pounds. She had a flat stomach, big ass, and DD breasts. She had a black weave that was bone straight and touched her ass.

"Are you going to come in, or are you going to stand in the doorway and stare at me all night? I would kind of preferred if you did more than stare," flirted Jade.

"Oh, my bad. Hey, beautiful," spoke Nathan.

"Hey, love," Jade replied as she led Nathan into her place.

"This looks nice. Do you live here by yourself?"

"No, I have a roommate, but she's out for the night, so we have the place all to ourselves. What would you like to drink?"

"I'll take a double shot of Patron."

"Alright, make yourself comfortable on the couch, and I got you."

Nathan went and sat on the couch and pulled his phone out. He sent Chloe a quick text, letting her know that he had made it to work like he always did. He had to make sure not to do anything out of the ordinary to make her suspicious. Jade handed Nathan the drink, and he knocked it back.

"Can I get one more?" Nathan asked.

"Sure," Jade replied as she got up from the couch and poured another drink but made sure to bring the bottle with her that time.

"Thank you," said Nathan as he took the shot from her hand.

"You're welcome, is everything okay?"

"Yeah, I'm good. No, I can't lie. I'm not okay."

"What's wrong? Talk to me, baby."

"I can't lie to you or string you along because in the end that will fuck me over. I have a wife at home, and I don't make it a habit of having drinks with naked women."

"Okay, I respect your honesty, but don't bullshit me. I don't care about you having a wife because I'm not trying to be your woman. I'm happy to live the single life. You knew what I was on when you decided to come over. I just jumped straight to the point. We good, we can have our fun whenever you want. No strings attached, just some good adult fun. You don't have to ever worry about me telling your wife. I know how to play my part. I could see you in the streets with her, and I'll walk past like I've never seen you before, so the ball is in your court."

Nathan sat there, looking at Jade's sexy lips, and he couldn't deny that he wanted to feel her lips wrapped around his dick. He figured one time wouldn't hurt. Nathan threw the shot back and stood from the couch.

"Alright, let's do this. Lead the way to your bedroom," said Nathan.

Jade took Nathan's hand and let him to her bedroom. She stripped him out of his clothes and slowly started kissing on his neck and pushed him back onto the bed. She could sense his hesitation, so she needed to make sure she stayed in control of the situation.

"Relax, I'll be gentle. At least the first time," purred Jade.

"This will be the only time, so we better make it count," replied Nathan.

Jade smirked at Nathan's words and began to trail kisses down his body until she made her way to his manhood. She sucked Nathan's balls then licked his shaft up and down before spitting a glob of spit on it. She took him into her mouth and a moan instantly escaped his lips as she went to work on his dick. He gripped the back of her head, and she bobbed up and down faster until slob dripped from her mouth.

Chloe barely gave Nathan oral, so he was welcoming the feeling that Jade was giving him. He felt his body tense up and knew that he was about to come. He tried to push her away, but she slapped his hand away and continued to suck until every drop of his cum seeped down her throat.

Jade looked Nathan in the eyes and smiled as she licked his cum off the sides of her lips. That sight alone had his shit back hard. Jade grabbed a condom from her nightstand and slid on his dick before sliding down on it.

"Damn," Jade moaned as she bounced up and down on his dick.

Nathan held onto her waist and pulled her farther down until she was taking every inch of him. "Just like that baby, come for me," Nathan whispered as she rubbed Jade's clit until she was coming on his dick.

Nathan and Jade continued to have sex for about another twenty minutes until he was cumming in the condom.

Nathan fell back on the bed, and Jade took the condom off and wrapped it up inside of a napkin.

"What time do you have to be home to your wife?"

Nathan looked over at the clock and saw that it was only ten thirty.

"I got about another hour before I need to be there."

"Well, I guess we need to make the time count," Jade said seductively before placing his dick back into her mouth.

Nathan and Jade went at it for two more rounds before he climbed out of bed and got dressed.

"Tonight, was fun," Nathan stated as Jade walked him to the door.

"Yeah, it was but next time, I'm going to have to charge you," Jade replied seriously.

"There's not going to be a next time. I already told you that."

"Yeah, okay, Nate. That's what they all say. I'll be ready when you want some more head, though." She smiled before kissing him on the cheek and letting him out of her house.

Nathan walked to his car and climbed in. He took his wedding band out of the cup holder and slipped back on his finger before driving home. When he made it home, all the lights were off, so he figured Chloe must have been in bed already since she had work the next morning. He extended up the stairs to his bedroom and found his wife knocked out. He walked as quietly as possible into the adjoining bathroom, so he wouldn't wake her. He didn't want her to smell the scent of another woman on his body.

Nathan stripped out of his clothes and stuffed them into the bottom of the hamper then turned the shower water on hot and climbed in. He scrubbed his body harder than usual because his conscience was eating at him already. He wanted to make sure that there was no trace of Jade left on him. He had just had the best sex in his life, and it wasn't with his wife. As bad as he wanted to only sleep with Jade once, he wasn't sure he'd be able to stick to that because the sex was just too good.

Nathan climbed out of the shower and dried off before going in his room and slipping on a pair of boxers and t-shirt. He climbed in bed, and Chloe began to stir in her sleep.

"You're back, was everything good?" mumbled Chloe.

"Yes, now go back to sleep," Nathan replied before kissing her on the forehead.

He closed his eyes and tried his best to fall asleep, but he just couldn't get his mind off of Jade. He didn't think that she would have that kind of effect on him because he had just met her. He knew the moment she wrapped her lips around his dick, his life would be changed forever.

❦ 7 ❧

J osh walked up to Iesha's door and rang the doorbell. He
  waited about a minute or so until she came and opened the
  door.

"Hey, baby," spoke Iesha.

"Hey, ma," Josh replied as he walked into Iesha's living room.

Iesha's house was styled to the T. From the outside, it looked
like shit, but the inside looked like it was out of one of those
homes magazines. She had the entire house coordinated in a red
and black color scheme.

"Do you want something to drink?"

"Nah, I'm good," Josh replied as he walked through the house
and went to one of the safes in Iesha's guest room.

Josh opened the safe and took out some of the dope, weed,
and his scale. He weighed what he needed and put it inside of
zip lock bags. It took him about thirty minutes to finish taking
care of his business. By the time he was done, he stuck everything in a backpack and put the other contents back inside of
the safe. When he walked into the living room, he found Iesha
sitting on the couch watching TV.

"Are you going to stay here with me tonight since we have to leave early in the morning? That way you won't have to make an extra trip."

"We're not leaving early in the morning. I'm leaving in about an hour," replied Josh.

"Why didn't you say anything? I could have been getting my bag ready."

"You're not going with me. That's why I haven't discussed any of the details with you about this trip. I'm going to be gone for about three days."

"So, who's going with you because I know you're not driving to Memphis by yourself."

"Tim, this girl named Bri, and Chyna. We have a few moves to make, but Tim wanted to take Bri since her birthday is coming up. Chyna is Bri's friend, so she was invited to celebrate with her."

Iesha looked at Josh like he was crazy before speaking. He knew the shit was coming once he mentioned Chyna's name, but he wasn't about to lie to her.

"Wow, so I get the overnight trips to Rockford while your new bitch gets weekend trips to Memphis."

"I keep telling you that's not my bitch. I haven't even had sex with the girl."

"Whatever nigga, if you haven't fucked her yet you trying very hard to. You are taking this bitch to dinners, movies, and all type of shit. Meanwhile, I'm just getting the late-night visits and looking stupid. Is the bitch even legal?"

"Yes, she's legal, and I don't know what to tell you, Iesha. You're sitting here tripping over nothing."

"I want you to tell me the fucking truth, Josh. Stop lying to me about that girl."

"I am telling you the truth, Iesha. It's not like me and you are together, so I don't have shit to hide. If I had sex with the girl and you asked, I would have told the truth like I've done when you asked about any other female. Chyna and I are just friends. I kick it with her, sometimes, but there's nothing serious going on between us."

Technically, Josh was telling the truth. He and Chyna had started hanging out more over the last couple of months after her return from Atlanta. They'd went out on a couple of dates and kissed. He had even given her head a few more times, but that was as far as she allowed it to go. It was his idea to take the girls to Memphis though. He wanted to be able to spend some time with her outside of her normal element and get her out of her comfort zone. He was hoping that she would see his efforts and finally give in and let him go further.

"You're so full of shit, Josh. I asked if you were willing to work on us getting back together, and you said yes. Yet, I don't see how if you're entertaining another bitch."

Josh rubbed his hands over his face to keep himself from losing his temper. He didn't to yell at her, but she was really starting to get on his nerve.

"I know what the fuck I told you. I also told you that I wanted to take it slow and build up what we had. It's not like I don't spend time with you, and I've tried to take you out and every time I try, you either pick a fight or end up canceling because you're busy in the streets."

"So, it's my fault that you trying to fuck that girl? You're saying that I don't give you enough attention now, Josh? Then tell that bitch she can't go or better yet if you aren't fucking with her like that then bring me with y'all, so that we can spend time together. After all, this is you new best friend, so if we're going to be in a relationship then I should be friends with her too."

"Look, chill out with this bullshit. I never said that anything was your fault," Josh said as he approached Iesha and pulled her into him.

"I swear, I can't stand your ass, Josh."

"I love you too, baby. I need to get up out of here though, so I'll text you when I get a chance."

"Damn, so I can't even get no dick before you go? We haven't been together in two days, and you about to gone for three."

"Oh, so that's why your problem is? You wanted the dick. You should have said that thirty minutes ago before this conversation even started, and I would have had time."

"Come on, I'm sorry. We can just have a quickie. I need to cum, baby," whined Iesha.

Josh looked down at his watch and saw that he needed to be at Tim's house in about forty minutes, so that meant he only had twenty minutes to spare. He really wasn't in the mood to fuck Iesha because of her temper tantrum, but he knew if he didn't give in to her, she would blow him up his entire trip.

Josh pulled down his pants, and Iesha wasted no time dropping down to her knees. She played in her love box while she bobbed her head up and down his dick. Once he was hard, he stopped her and pulled her shorts down. He bent her over the arm of the couch and entered her from the back. He slapped her ass and dug in deep. He watched as her cream coated his dick. He grabbed a handful of her hair and fucked her until she was squirting on his dick. After a few more pumps, he was coming right behind her.

Josh held onto Iesha waste for a few more seconds, then pulled out of her and went into the bathroom. He grabbed a washcloth and cleaned his dick off than pulled his clothes up and joined Iesha in the living room.

"You calm now?" Josh asked as he picked up the backpack from the bed.

"A little, I would have been better if you gave me head or something."

"I got you when I get back. You know I'm on a time limit, so it had to be quick."

"I know, I love you and be safe," said Iesha.

"I will, and I love you too," Josh replied as he walked out of the house.

Josh walked to his car and sent Tim a message, letting him

know that he was on his way. He was trying to stick to the schedule he made because they had a nine-hour drive. He just hoped Chyna was at Bri's house already and they were ready to go.

Josh pulled up to Tim's house then blew the horn. Tim immediately came out of the house, and they headed in the direction of Bri's house. Josh had Tim shoot Bri a text, letting her know they needed to be ready because they were almost there. By the time Josh made it to Bri's house, the girls were already standing on the porch with their luggage.

Josh smiled as Chyna and Bri walked towards his truck. Chyna wore a short white sundress and a pair of white sandals. Everyone spoke to each other and the girls climbed into the truck. Tim got in the backseat with Bri, and Chyna climbed into the front seat while Josh drove.

"You look beautiful, baby," complimented Josh.

"Thank you," replied Chyna

"You know I can't believe that you're actually going. When I asked you, I just knew that you weren't going to be able to go," said Josh.

"Believe me, it wasn't easy. My family definitely doesn't know that you and Tim are going. They know I'm with Bri for her birthday, but they weren't about to let me go with just her, so they think her cousin and his girlfriend is going as well. With the help of my brother and the guilt trip, I convinced them to let me go. Plus, I told them that I start school in a few weeks, so I at least wanted to do one trip for the summer."

"Well, I'm just glad that you were able to convince them. I've been looking forward to spending some real quality time with you."

"I've been looking forward to it as well."

Josh and Chyna talked for almost the entire four hours that he drove. They stopped and grabbed gas and some snacks. When they got back to the truck, Josh and Chyna had swapped spots with Tim and Iesha then was back on the road.

Josh pulled Chyna close to him, and she laid her head on his shoulder. She was a little cold, so she grabbed her throw and put it over her lap.

"Do you have on underwear?" Josh asked as he laid his hand on Chyna's thigh.

"Yes, I have on a thong," whispered Chyna.

Josh slid his hand up Chyna's dress until he felt her honey pot. He started rubbing it slowly, catching her off guard. She tried to grab his arm to stop, but he pushed her hand away and started sucking on her neck.

"Just relax and stay quiet. They won't even know what we're doing. They can't see my hand because you're covered up."

"I know that, but what about your seat and my dress?"

Josh bent over and unzipped his gym bag then pulled a dry towel out of the bag.

"Raise up a little," Josh said as he put the towel on the seat and lifted her dress up, so she was sitting directly on the towel.

Chyna sat back down and leaned her head on Josh's shoulder and allowed him to play in love pot until she was cumming all on his hands. He pulled his hand from up under her dress and licked his fingers with one by one.

It was no doubt in Chyna's mind that she was going to fuck Josh on the Memphis trip, but the freaky shit that he had just done, made it worth it for her. If he could make her cum like that with his fingers and mouth, she could only imagine what his dick could do to her. He had been very patient with her, so she was ready.

❄ 8 ❄

The group made it to Memphis around nine o'clock the next morning. Josh and Tim did an early check-in at The Westin. They climbed onto the elevator and took it to the top floor. Josh and Chyna went into their room while Tim and Bri went into the room a couple doors down. Chyna walked inside and looked around. She must admit; she was surprised with Josh's taste. She was used to fancy hotels and renting out houses, but she didn't expect that from Josh. His taste had her impressed. They were staying in the King Executive suite. It had a king bed, one and a half baths with a whirlpool in one of the bathrooms.

"Baby, why don't you order us some breakfast from room service? I need to make a few calls right quick," said Josh.

Chyna picked up the menu and dialed the phone number for room service. She ordered two turkey sausage omelets with grits, toast, and orange juice. Once she finished ordering food, she pulled her phone to call Rome and let him know that she made it. She had already called her parents when they first made it to the hotel.

"Hello," Rome answered on the second ring, sounding halfway asleep.

"Hey, you're still sleep?"

"I was, I had business to take care of last night, so I didn't get home until almost five this morning."

"Awe okay, I was just calling to let you now I made it."

"Okay, you be careful. Do you have enough money because I can transfer some to your account?"

"No, I'm good, dad gave me some money before I left. I'm also going to see Uncle Ray while I'm out here, and he said he had something for me."

"Alright, I love you. Make sure to text me later."

"I love you too, and I will," Chyna replied before hanging up the phone.

Chyna laid across the bed and balled up while Josh finished his phone calls. She laid there for about ten minutes until there was a knock at the door. She knew it had to be the food she ordered. Chyna went in the bathroom and washed her hands while Josh got the food. She walked into the dining room area of the suite and took a seat at the table with Josh.

"We have to leave around noon for a meeting, so I'm going to take a nap and shower. I'm not sure how long we'll be gone for. I'm going to leave some money for you, so that you can go shopping if you want to. We're having dinner on the rooftop at the Majestic Grille."

"Okay, that'll work for me. I want to take a nap as well," replied Chyna.

Chyna and Josh finished their breakfast then climbed into bed. They snuggled under each other and fell asleep. Chyna didn't know how long she had been sleeping, but she heard a knock at the door, and the bed was empty.

Chyna climbed out of the bed and stretched her legs than went to the door and opened it. She looked through the peephole and saw that it was Bri.

"Hey, girl, I been trying to call you. What's wrong with your phone?"

"I was sleep, and I never turned my ringtone back on."

"Awe, okay, so what do you want do?"

"I want to go get a Brazilian wax."

"Ohhhh, a wax huh? Somebody finally ready?"

"Yeah, tonight is going to be the night. I want my entire body smooth as butter."

"Okay, I see you, hun. Well, let's get out of here and get it done. We can even go get massages as well."

"Alright, just let me take a quick shower first."

Chyna walked into the bathroom and took a shower than grabbed a pair of black biker shorts and a white tank top with a pair of sandals. She combed her hair into a ponytail, looked on the dresser, and grabbed the money Josh had left for her. It had to have been about three thousand dollars. She grabbed her purse and phone and left out of the room with Bri following right behind her.

Chyna and Bri walked out of the house and headed to European Wax Center where Chyna got her entire body waxed. When it got to her lady business, Chyna was ready to jump from the table from the pain she felt. Once they finished at the wax center, they went to Relax H2O Inc. They decided to try the aqua massage. It was a machine similar as a tanning bed. All you had to do was take your shoes off and climb inside. The machine is filled with water and a barrier is in the middle, stopping you from being in the actual water. It was a way of getting a full boy massage without someone having to touch you.

Chyna and Bri finished up at the spa and decided to go look at some of the boutiques in the area. They both found a couple of cute little outfits that they liked. They both already had clothes to wear for dinner, so they were just getting stuff for the fun of it. By the time they finished and made it back to the hotel, Josh and Tim were already back. They were sitting on the balcony of Josh's hotel, smoking.

Chyna walked onto the balcony, and Josh pulled Chyna onto his lap.

"Did you have fun shopping?"

"A little, I didn't really do much shopping. We went to the spa and got massages and went to get waxes."

"Oh, what did you get waxed?"

"I'll show you later," smiled Chyna.

"Yo, y'all get out," joked Josh.

"Don't listen to him. You don't have to go anywhere."

Josh handed Chyna the blunt, and she inhaled a couple puffs before handing it over to Bri. They all sat on the balcony and talked for about an hour until Tim and Bri left to go to their room.

"I'm about to go lay down for about an hour. Do you need anything?" asked Josh.

"No, you can take your nap. I'm going to need about two hours to get dressed. I have to do my hair and make-up."

"Alright, well just make sure you wake me up in time to shower and get dressed."

"Okay, I will."

Chyna walked into the bathroom and took a shower. Once she finished, she started curling her hair. She did it in a loose curl, so that it would flow once they fell. She then woke Josh up and started on her make-up. About fifteen minutes later, she heard the bathroom door open. She watched him through the mirror as he walked out in with nothing but a towel. He took his underwear from the suitcase and dropped his towel. Chyna's eyes bugged at the sight of his manhood. She had never even seen Josh shirtless before, and now she was seeing his full package. He knew he was a decent size because she would feel it while sitting on his lap. She was starting to get nervous about the night because he was packing, and he wasn't even hard. She couldn't believe that was going to spend entire weekend with him.

"You like what you see?" Josh asked as he walked over to her.

"Yeah, your body is sexy," Chyna replied.

"Thank you, baby. I can show you what this body can do you right now, if you want."

The looks in Chyna's eyes were telling him to do it, but the words never escaped her mouth.

"We have to finish getting ready for dinner," Chyna said nervously.

Josh gave her a knowingly look before smirking. "Okay, you're right. I'm just going to finish getting dressed and make a call."

"Alright," was all Chyna could say because her nerves were getting the best of her.

Chyna finished her make-up and slipped on her black lace panties with a black strapless lace bra. She slipped her white Versace S&M dress over her head. It was a buckled strapped knee-length dress. The buckle wrapped around her neck and connected to the front of the dress. It had a slim fit and showed off her curves. She slipped a pair of red Christian Louboutin Pigalle Follies leather pumps. She stood and looked at the mirror and couldn't help but admire her own body. The pumps had her legs looking longer, and the dress against her skin made her look curvier.

Chyna grabbed her red Lou bag from off the desk and walked to join Josh in the living room.

"Damn!" Josh exclaimed as he examined Chyna's body from head to toe.

He knew that she had style from the times he had hung out with her, but he had never seen her dressed up before. She could go from rocking a pair of leggings and white one to Versace and red bottoms.

"I take that as a compliment. You look good too," Chyna complimented him. He had on a black pair of slacks with a dress shirt, tie, and vest.

"Thanks, ma, are you ready to go? Tim and Bri will meet us in the lobby."

"Yeah, I'm ready," replied Chyna.

Chyna and Josh exited the room and walked to the elevator;

just as they were getting on, Tim and Bri were getting on behind them.

"Damn, Chy, I keep telling you. You need to start a class on how you got your body like that. You look good as hell," said Bri.

"Thanks, Bri, you look good too. I already told you I can't be out here giving away game," giggled Chyna.

The group walked outside, and the valet brought Josh's car around. They climbed inside and headed to the restaurant. They were halfway to the restaurant when Chyna's phone started to ring. She looked down at it and saw that it was her uncle.

"Hey," Chyna spoke into the phone.

"Hey, what time will you be ready tomorrow? Your aunt wants to make sure she has food done."

"I told you that she didn't have to do that, and you can send the car around three. I'm going to lunch and the museum tomorrow, first."

"Alright, be careful out here. I told your father I'd look out for you if you need me."

"I know, but I'm good. I'll see you tomorrow," Chyna said before hanging up the phone.

"Is everything okay?" Josh asked, getting Chyna's attention.

"Yeah, that was my uncle calling to check on me. I promised him that I'd visit while I was here," replied Chyna.

The group pulled up to the Majestic Grille, and Josh gave the car to valet while they entered the restaurant. He checked in with the hostess and they led them up to the rooftop dining. Chyna loved the view because the city had a beautiful glow about it at night.

"Here's your menus, your waiter should be here shortly," the hostess stated before walking away.

The waiter walked over to the group a few minutes later, and Josh ordered a bottle of Merlot for the table, then everyone placed their dinner orders.

When the bottle came to the table, Chyna drunk a glass of wine faster than usual, piquing Bri's attention.

"Chy, I have to go to the restroom. Will you come with me so you can help me with my dress?" asked Bri.

"Sure," Chyna replied as she stood from the table and walked with Bri to the restroom.

"Okay, spill, what's wrong? Did you have sex with Josh, and you didn't enjoy it or something?"

"No, it's not that. We didn't have sex yet. When we got back to the room, he took a nap and showered while I did my hair and got dressed."

"Alright, so what's the problem?"

"I'm just nervous as hell about tonight."

"Look, you have nothing to be nervous about. If you're not ready, he has to respect that. If he can't respect that, then he's not the one for you to give your V-card to," Bri said sincerely.

"It's not that, I know that I'm ready or I wouldn't even be entertaining the idea. It's just I saw him naked as his stuff is big. What if It doesn't fit or he doesn't enjoy it? I know he has a lot of experience under his belt."

Bri let out a light chuckle before responding. "No matter what size it is, it'll fit. It's going to take some time for your body to adjust to it in the beginning, but once he finally gets in there--if he knows what he's doing--you'll start enjoying it. It doesn't matter how much experience he has. You're young, tight, and can get wet. Having sex with you will probably feel better than any sex he's ever had. Just make sure that you let him know that you're still a virgin before you actually let him try to stick it in. If you don't tell him, he might be so anxious because you made him wait so long, and he might try to rush into it."

"Thanks, Bri, you just don't know how much I appreciate you."

"You're welcome, you're my best friend, and I'll always be here for you," smiled Bri.

After the conversation with Bri, Chyna was feeling much better and confident about the situation. They washed their hands and headed back to the table with the men.

"We thought we were going to have to come find y'all. Everything good?" asked Tim.

"Yeah, we just had to have a little girl talk," replied Bri.

The waiter brought the food out, and they all ate and had a good time. Even though the guys were older than them, they still had a lot to talk about, and the dinner was enjoyable. Once the dinner was over, they paid the bill and went for a stroll on the Riverwalk. Josh was impressed that Chyna wanted to go for a walk in three-inch heels. He was used to women complaining about their feet hurting just from having them on for a few minutes. He made a mental note to talk to her and find out more about the lifestyle she lived. He could tell that she still had things she hadn't told him, but he would never knock her for that because she didn't know everything about him either.

❦ 9 ❦

C hyna and Josh walked into their suite and headed to the bedroom. They put their things down, then Chyna headed to the bathroom to wash her face and brush her teeth. After she washed her face, she brushed her hair into a ponytail and stripped out of her dress. She took a deep breath before leaving out of the bathroom and joining Josh in the bedroom.

Josh was sitting on the bed doing something on the phone until he heard Chyna clear her throat.

Josh looked up and couldn't do anything but smile. He could tell through clothes that Chyna's body was banging, but without clothes, it was even more beautiful. He tossed his phone on the bed then stood and walked over to her. He wasted no time pulling her close to him and ramming his lips into hers. He bit on the bottom of her lip then slid his tongue into her mouth, tasting the Colgate toothpaste on her tongue. His hand roamed down and gripped a handful of her ass. He pushed her gently onto the bed before stripping down to his boxers. He looked over in his bag and grabbed the box of magnums he had bought and sat them on the nightstand.

Josh climbed back in the bed and started kissing Chyna passionately, only stopping to unclasp her bra and toss it to the side. He kissed her from her neck to her breast. While sucking on one breast, he used his hand to massage the other one. He took turns paying both breasts attention. Josh allowed his tongue to make a trail down her body. He took his time kissing and rubbing all over her entire body. He pulled her underwear off and tossed them as well.

"Damn, you're so fucking beautiful," Josh growled before lying flat on the bed and dipping his tongue into her honey spot.

Chyna closed her eyes and gripped the back of her head, welcoming the sensation his tongue was causing her body. He licked and sucked on her pussy until her body started to shake and convulse. She held his head tighter, and she rode the wave of ecstasy until she was coming in his mouth.

Josh came up for air and took off his boxers, then slid her legs back open with his knee. He used the tip of his dick and rubbed it on her clit, causing a moan to escape her lips. He could feel that she was dripping wet and he could only imagine how it was about to feel to bury himself deep within her thighs. He slid his dick down to her opening, and she stopped him.

"Wait, there's something I need to tell you," said Chyna.

Josh prayed that she wasn't about to say she changed her mind after she had got him all the way riled up. All the times he gave her head, he knew what to expect because he never got naked and all she did was take her pants off. Plus, she would always tell him that she wasn't about to fuck him, even if he ate her out. This time, she didn't give that indication, so he thought it was a go.

"Let me guess, you don't want to do this?" Josh asked, not even bothering to hide his frustration.

"It's not that. I'm ready to have sex with you. I just thought that you should know that I'm still a virgin before we do it," replied Chyna.

Josh looked Chyna in the eyes to see if she was joking, but she never even cracked a smile. All the time he had been talking to her, she never mentioned never having sex before. He just figured she wasn't easy and wanted to get to know him before putting out. He knew that she was young, but he also knew a lot of girls that was busting it open at fifteen and sixteen years old.

"Okay, are you sure you're ready because I won't be mad if you say no. I would never force you into doing something that you'll regret later."

"I'm sure, just take your time, please."

"I will, I promise," Josh replied before kissing her passionately.

He slid his hand down between her legs and began to rub on her clit. He slid his fingers down and stuck one inside of her then another, trying to loosen her up a little and causing her to wince. Whenever he had given her head, he never stuck his fingers inside of her. The most he had done with his hand was rub the clit while he ate because he hadn't fingered a girl since high school. Once he saw that she was coming again, he moved his fingers and began to slide the head in.

"Arrgggh," Chyna cried out as she gripped the top of his shoulders to stop him.

"Shit," Josh groaned from the feeling of her tightness.

He hadn't even put it all the way in yet, and she had him feeling like he was ready to cum. He began rubbing on her clit some more to try to get her to calm down. Once she was moaning again, he thrust his dick completely inside of her, causing her to scream out in pain. Tears instantly fell from her eyes.

Josh went in and out of her slowly as he kissed her tears away. He had been fantasizing about fucking her for three months and never did he think it would feel the way it did. Words could not explain how good her pussy felt wrapped around her dick. He had sex with more women than he could remember but none of them felt as good as Chyna. After about five minutes, her moans of pain turned into moans of pleasure as she wrapped one of her legs around his waist, causing him to go even deeper.

"Oh my, God, Josh. I think I'm about to cum, baby!" Chyna screamed out.

Josh groaned as he picked up the pace some. By that time, Chyna had both legs in the air without Josh even having to hold them for her. He never knew she was that flexible, but he loved every bit of it. He bit down on his bottom lip to keep from screaming like a bitch.

"You feel so fucking good, baby. This my shit now," Josh growled into her ear as he punished her pussy.

Chyna's body began to shake as she came on his dick. The gush felt so good that it caused him to come right behind her, burying his seeds deep inside of her. He knew it was stupid to fuck without a condom, and he didn't make a habit of that. Iesha was the only girl that he went in raw with. He just couldn't help it with Chyna though. She was pure and untouched; no other man had been there before, so he knew that she was clean.

"Did you cum?" asked Chyna.

"Yeah, I did. I promise I don't normally cum that quick, but your shit felt so damn good. I'm surprised I lasted as long as I did. You had me ready to bust before I was even all the way in."

"I'm not complaining, I was just wondering because you stopped moving but still laying on top of me."

"Oh, yeah, I'm not done with you yet. I was just giving you time to catch your breath," Josh smirked before kissing her lips. Once his felt his dick getting all the way back hard, he rolled over onto his back, making sure to stay inside of her. He needed at least one more round, and he knew if he pulled out, she was not about to let him back him.

"Let me teach you how to ride it," Josh said as he lifted Chyna up and down, slowly on his dick. It only took a few minutes for her to catch on before she was riding him like a pro. He could tell that she had to have enjoyed dancing because she in there twerking on his dick.

They went at it for about another thirty minutes, alternating positions that didn't require him pulling out before he dropped another load inside of her. He laid on top of her for a couple of minutes to catch his breath then got up from the bed and went into the bathroom to turn the whirlpool on. He came back into the bedroom and found Chyna still laying in the same exact spot.

Josh picked Chyna up out of the bed and placed her inside of the hot water. He knew that her body had to be aching from the beating he had put on it.

"Sit here and soak while I go change the covers," suggested Josh. They had only had sex on top of the blanket, but there was a little blood on it, so he wanted to make sure it hadn't gone through the blanket.

Once he finished taking the blanket from the bed, he walked back into the bathroom and climbed into the whirlpool with Chyna, where she was allowing the jets to massage her body. She looked up at Josh and smiled before he pulled her over to him and began to massage her shoulders.

"Hmmm, that feels so good," moaned Chyna.

Chyna and Josh stayed in the whirlpool for another twenty minutes before they went to get in bed. Josh laid down and pulled Chyna into her arms. She threw one leg over him and nestled her head into his chest until they both had fallen asleep.

The following morning, Chyna woke up to an empty bed and the smell of food. She climbed out of bed and put on a robe than walked into the living area where she found Josh sitting in a chair. She was about to walk past him, but he pulled her close to him instead and sat her on the table.

"Good morning, beautiful," said Josh.

"Good morning," replied Chyna.

Josh leaned in and kissed Chyna on the lips before sliding his hand up her robe. He felt that she was naked and smiled before lifting one of her legs and throwing it over his shoulder. He wasted no time diving in headfirst.

"Hmmm, that feels so good, Josh. Don't stop, baby, just like that," Chyna moaned. He continued to devour her until she was cumming in his mouth.

He lifted her from the table and turned around. He pulled his dick from his box and attempted to enter her from the back. She tensed up a little but relaxed as he pushed it all the way in.

"Fuck," Josh groaned as his dick slid in and out of her from the back.

Her cream had his manhood coated white. He smiled at the sight of his dick going in and out of her. She gripped the edge of the table and threw her ass back on him. He could already tell he was going to have fun with Chyna. She hadn't been around the block, so he could train and teach her to fuck him the same way he'd did Iesha. Iesha wasn't a virgin when he met her, but after fucking with her for years, he taught her how to please him, and now she fucked him like a porn star. It was only a matter of time before he had Chyna the same way.

Once Chyna and Josh finished their sex session, they ate the food Josh ordered from room service then took a shower and got dressed. Chyna brushed her hair into a ponytail and put on a coat of lip gloss. After that, she sent her family a text to check-in. it was already noon, so they exited the room and met Tim and Bri in the lobby then headed across the street to The Memphis Rock 'n' Soul Museum.

Everyone walked around the Museum and looked at all the different exhibits. They stayed for about an hour and a half then went and had lunch at Gus's World-Famous Fried Chicken.

"So, what do you ladies have planned this evening while we're working?" asked Tim.

"We're going to Chyna's family house," replied Bri.

"Awe, what part of Memphis does your family stay?"

"They have a house in Germantown," said Chyna.

"Oh, your people got money," responded Tim.

"Something like that," Chyna stated, brushing off Tim's response. She still wasn't about to indulge anything pertaining to her family to them. She wasn't stupid; that's why her father wanted her to be with someone familiar within the organization, so that it wouldn't be compromised, so she knew she had to be extra careful."

"Do you need us to give you a ride, so that you don't have to take a cab?" asked Josh.

Chyna was about to reply just as her phone dinged. She looked down at it and saw that it was a message from her cousin, letting her know to be ready in ten minutes.

"Oh shit, no, thank you. We have to go, my ride will be outside the hotel in ten minutes," said Chyna.

The group paid the tab and got up from the table. Luckily, the restaurant was only five minutes away from their hotel, but she knew it was a big chance that they would be pulling up at the same time as her cousin. If he saw Chyna with the guys, it was over with for her because he was definitely going to tell Rome.

They pulled up to the hotel, and Chyna jumped out of the car but bumped right into her cousin, Ron.

"Hey, baby cuz," Ron greeted her as he pulled her into the hug.

"Hey, big cuz," Chyna replied as she returned the hug.

After looking at Chyna and Ron, you could see the family resemblance. All of their family had the same color skin, eyes, and dark black hair. No matter if they were male or female, young or old.

"You could've told me you weren't back yet. I wasn't going to rush you."

"I know, but I didn't want you stuck out here waiting. Uncle Ray didn't even tell me you were coming. I thought you were moving to ATL."

"It was a surprise, I'm actually moving next month. We decided to push it back a month since Maddox has to come out there and help situate his brother first."

"Oh okay, well I'm ready to go. Bri is going with us."

Ron looked in the direction of whom was standing by Tim and Josh on the other side of him.

Ron gave Chyna a knowing look but kept quiet. He would

never embarrass her in public, but once they were alone, she was going to hear his mouth.

"What's up, y'all," spoke Ron.

"What's up," replied the guys.

Bri kissed Tim on the lips then walked over to where Chyna and Ron were standing. Chyna excused herself for a minute and walked over to Josh.

"I'm about to get out of here now. I'll text you when we make it back. I should only be a few hours."

"Okay, if you need anything just let me know."

Chyna nodded her head okay and walked away. She and Josh weren't in a relationship, and they never kissed in public, so she wasn't about to pretend now just because they had sex.

"Can I drive, Ron?"

"Yeah, but this isn't no rental like that Lambo in ATL, so drive my shit right," warned Ron.

"Alright, I will," laughed Chyna.

Chyna jumped in the driver's seat of the White Bentley truck and took off in the direction of her uncle's house.

Chyna and Bri spent the evening laughing and talking to her family. Chyna really enjoyed visiting them. They were the aunt and uncle her father always threatened to send her to. The threat wasn't because it was bad there; it was because they lived in a quiet area, and they figured it would slow me down. Little did they know, she had no problem finding out how to get around, and she could definitely make her way to Memphis' hood.

It was almost nine, so Chyna and Bri were getting ready to go.

"I am so glad you came to visit us. Good luck in college, and if you need anything let me know. Here's your birthday and graduation present together. It's from me, your aunt, and cousin," Uncle Ray said as he handed Chyna a Neiman Marcus bag. Inside of the bag was a black Prada backpack along with a Prada brim hat.

"Oh, this is nice, unc. I love it. Thank you," Chyna replied as she hugged him.

"You're welcome, but the main gift is inside of the Prada bag," informed Ray.

Chyna opened the backpack and pulled a card out. Her aunt, uncle, and cousin had signed the card. She flipped over the check, and her eyes grew big as saucers. She couldn't believe they had given her twenty thousand dollars.

"Wait, what is this for? This is way too much money," replied Chyna.

"Look, you're eighteen now, and I know my brother is strict, but he means well. I just want to give you this as a backup plan if you ever may need one. Just put it in your bank account and use it wisely."

"Oh, my God, I love you so much," Chyna gleamed as she hugged her uncle.

"I love you, too," replied Ray.

Chyna hugged her aunt and uncle goodbye then went to join her cousin and Bri out at his car.

"Do you like your gifts?" asked Ron.

"Yes, I love you guys so much," said Chyna.

"We love you more, princess. You know we need to talk real quick before I drop you off, though."

"Yeah, I know," Chyna replied as she walked away with Ron, out of Bri's earshot. Even though her and Bri were best friends, it was somethings that she didn't even know about Chyna's family. It wasn't that she didn't trust her. She wanted to protect Bri, in case her family ever got caught up in some shit.

"Who is those guys y'all were with at the hotel? I know you didn't just meet them, or they wouldn't have been at your hotel because you're smarter than that."

"Those are a couple friends of Bri and I."

"Friends as in your boyfriend?"

"No, he's only my friend. I don't have a boyfriend right now."

"Okay, I can't tell you, what you can and can't do. All I can tell you is to be careful. If you ever get uncomfortable around them or they seem shady, you need to let Rome know. Looking at them, I can tell they from the streets."

"I will, and I won't even tell you not to say anything, but could you please at least just tell Rome? I don't want your dad or my father finding out right now."

"Alright, I will only tell Rome. Text me tomorrow when you make it home, then I'll tell him, so that way he doesn't ruin your last night here. If I tell him now, he'll be trying to catch a flight here," laughed Ron.

"Yeah, I know. I appreciate that, big cuz," said Chyna.

Ron drove Chyna and Bri back to the hotel. Tim and Josh were already back, so the ladies went in and changed their clothes then headed to Beale Street. Chyna nor Bri was old enough to be there, but with Tim and Josh's pull, they got them through. They spent the remainder of the night drinking and walking around until they went back to the hotel because they were leaving out early the next morning to head home.

❧ 10 ❧

Chyna was laying across her bed reading *The 48 Laws of Power* by Robert Greene when her phone went off. She looked down at the text and saw a message from Rome, letting her know that he was outside.

Chyna closed her book and climbed out of her bed. She grabbed her gym bag and headed down the stairs. She was at home alone, so she didn't have to worry about anybody stopping her.

"Hey, big head," Chyna spoke as she climbed into the car.

"Hey, baby girl," replied Rome.

Rome and Chyna were on their way to the gym for her routine workout and range shooting. They did their thirty minutes of shooting then went to work out. Chyna was just waiting on him to bring up Josh because she knew it was coming. She had been back in town for a week, and she knew Ron had already told him. Surprisingly, they got through the entire workout and run without saying anything. Once they finished at the gym, they took showers and headed out to find something to eat at Chili's. Rome and Chyna were seen to their seats, and they ordered because they already knew what they wanted.

"I'm sorry that I didn't come get you, yesterday like I was

74

supposed to. We just been extra busy. We might need Maddox and his crew to come out here sooner than we expected," Rome said, breaking the silence.

"Speaking of business being busy, I think it was about time that I start helping out when I'm not busy with school."

"You know you don't have to do that. Pops will give you an allowance until you're twenty-one."

"I know, but I don't want to have to depend on that. I want to make my own money, so that I'll have enough saved up just in case they decide they don't want to pay my rent next year."

"They won't do that, and if they do, then I'll pay it for you."

"It's not the same, Rome. I'm already stuck living in the house, so I want to at least make my own money. I need to find some sense of independence. This shit is driving me crazy because the plan was always for me to be out on my own when I turned eighteen."

"Okay, think about which business you want to help out with, and I'll talk to pops about getting you in."

"I already know the business I want to help out in. I want to do distribution," said Chyna.

"What, are you out of your mind? I can already tell you the answer is no. Find something else to do, Chy. Does this have anything to do with that nigga, Josh, you been running around with?"

"First of all, no, I'm not out of mind. I've been studying, and I know I can do this. You've been doing this with them since you were sixteen. Oh, what since I have a vagina, I can't be a part of it? This has nothing to do with him and you know it. I've always had my own mind and working a nine to five has never been in my books. The only reason I'm going to school is to build the craft for my business."

Rome rubbed his hand over his face out of frustration before responding to his sister. "Look Chy, I know all about him. You know my ears is always to the street. I've heard about you running around with him way before Ron called and told me that day. I just didn't say anything because I was waiting on the right time. Since you lied and went all the way to Memphis with him, I know it's serious. Did you deliver drugs for him?"

Chyna looked around to make sure nobody could hear them, but luckily, they were sitting in the back corner of the restaurant, and it was fairly empty. She was about to reply but saw the waitress coming with their orders, so she waited for her to place the food on the table and walk away.

"I am not stupid, Rome. I didn't deliver no damn drugs for him. I'm not familiar with nobody in Memphis but our family that's there, and I'm definitely not delivering shit for nobody for free. I'm not going to lie; him and his boy had some business to take care of out there. Bri and I just kicked it with them when they weren't working. I didn't go to any meetings or any part of the hood. I don't even know who they saw and what they actually delivered. I've never even been around any of his drugs. As far as he knows, I'm just an innocent eighteen-year-old girl on her way to college. I mean, I'm sure he knows who you all are by now since I've been in public with him. So, people are probably whispering in his ear the same way they are yours, but he thinks I'm naïve when it comes to that lifestyle. I don't talk to him about anything that has to do with what our family does, so he only knows what everybody else in the streets know."

"So, how serious are you two? You call yourself seeing a future with him?"

"We're not serious at all. He's not even my boyfriend. Josh and I are only friends."

"Only friends, huh? Are you having sex with him?"

"Do you really want to know that answer, Rome?"

"You don't even have to answer it, Chy, because I already know the answer. You were with him for an entire weekend away, so I'm not naïve enough to think that you didn't do anything. I don't want to think about my little sister out here having sex, but I knew that you weren't going to be a virgin forever, and I know I can't pick and choose who you date. You're eighteen now, and you're smart. All I can do is give you some advice when it comes to dating older street niggas. Keep your eyes open and protect your heart."

"I am, Rome, I don't even know where it's going to go with us. Just because I slept him doesn't mean I'm in love with him now and about to rush into a relationship. It was just sex, and we're going to take things one day at a time. I can't really care less about a relationship. I'm trying to get money and live my life like I was meant to be."

Rome looked in his sister eyes and chuckled because she reminded him so much of himself. She was a female version of him, and that was dangerous for any nigga that fucked with her. Typically, they would warn the female about getting they heart broke, but when it came to Chyna, they would have to warn the man to protect his heart from her.

"It's like this, Chyna. I want to help you out, but it's dangerous out here in these streets. Can you at least think about doing something else? You can be a secretary at one of the properties and work your own hours. It won't even feel like a nine to five."

Chyna leaned back in her seat and looked at her brother. She was trying to find the right words to say what was on her mind, but the only thing she could do was keep it real like she'd always done.

"I'm not about to bullshit you, Rome. I'm eighteen now and old enough to make my own decisions as well as mistakes. You and dad can only shelter me from the streets for so long. The hustle is running through my veins. I have the same amount of urge to get this money as I do to breathe. I came to you first because you're family and what our family does. If you're not comfortable with me doing it, I can respect that. However, that doesn't change the fact that I'm still going to do it. I already know someone else that's willing to get me to the right people that I need to see. I'm even in the process of getting my workers together. I already have the money that I need."

"Look, Chyna, please don't rush to do anything. Give me a chance to talk to pops and see what he says. If it's a flat no, I'll allow you to do you until he comes around."

"Alright, I'll give you one week. I appreciate you looking out for me Rome. I really do but you know how you were at my age, and I have that same drive."

"Yeah, I know baby girl, don't stress it. Let's finish our dinner then I'll take you home."

Chyna and Rome finished eating their meals then he drove her back home while he went to take care of some business.

Chyna went up to her room and read her book. She really hoped that her brother could convince her father because she didn't want to get money outside of the family, but if she had to, then she would. She was going to become a boss bitch by any means necessary.

🙰🙵

JOSH SAT ON HIS COUCH AND LISTENED TO IESHA NAG. SHE had been nagging ever since he told her it was alright for her to come over. If he hadn't needed the work she had for him, he would have let her stay where she was.

"Do you hear me talking to you, Josh?"

"Yes, I hear you, but what the fuck do you want me to say? I told your ass I been busy since I got back in town."

"Yeah, I bet you not too busy for your other bitch, though."

"What the fuck is you talking about, Iesha? I haven't seen that damn girl since we made it back from Memphis. I've been busy working, not thinking about no pussy!" snapped Josh.

Josh was somewhat telling the truth. He hadn't seen Chyna since they got back, but that was all because of her. He tried to get her to come over to see him a couple of days ago, but she claimed she was busy getting things together for school but would make time for him soon. He couldn't believe that she was actually avoiding him. That was new for him because he was used to women sweating him after they had sex. He knew that she enjoyed it because she even initiated the sex the last night they were there. He thought she'd still be tired from the night before, but she proved him wrong.

"Yeah, aight. Well, I heard she was out laughing and grinning in some nigga's face over dinner today."

"I don't give a fuck; she can do whatever she wants. I'm not in a relationship with her!" yelled Josh.

"I bet, you fucked her, though didn't you?"

"Yes, I had sex with Chyna while in Memphis. She shared a room with me that weekend, and we had sex for the first time. Is that what you wanted to hear?"

"I swear, I can't stand your ass. You so fucking trifling. I knew you were going to fuck that bitch. That's why I only heard from you once while you were there then you blocked me the rest of the trip," cried Iesha.

"Please, don't start with this crying shit. I'm not in the mood for it today. I have a headache, which is why I had you come to me and not the other way around."

"You're so fucking insensitive, sometimes. Had that been me doing what you're doing, it'd be a problem."

"Actually, it wouldn't, did you forget that you were doing it while we were together or that you were just fucking with some-body else the beginning of this year? I didn't trip about it. I allowed you to do you because that's what we agreed on. You have no room to get mad. I don't question you, so if you stopped questioning me, your feelings wouldn't get hurt."

"Yes, it would because people know I fuck with you, and they be coming to me about you."

"Well, tell they ass to mind they own business or better yet, stop having them think we're in a relationship then they wouldn't feel the need to tell you my business," Josh stated as he laid back on his couch.

"Can I stay here with you tonight, Josh? I don't mean to nag, I just miss you. I know I have to stop tripping because we're not back in a relationship yet, and I'll allow you to get shorty out of your system, but I'm not going to stick around and wait forever, for you to decide if you want me or not."

"I told you my head hurt, Esh. I'm not in the mood for sex, and I know that's what you want."

"We can just go up to your room, and I can give you some head to help relax you then we can just cuddle and go to sleep. Please? I promise not to bring that girl back up, tonight," pleaded Iesha.

Josh thought about it for a minute and figured, what the hell. He hadn't busted a nut in a week, and he could go for some head.

Iesha and Josh walked up to his bedroom, and he laid across his bed. She pulled his dick out of his basketball shorts and went to town on him. It took her about twenty minutes then he was cumming in her mouth. He watched as she swallowed every drop before stripping down to her underwear and lying in bed next to him.

Iesha remained true to her word and laid quietly with him until they both started dosing off. His phone started ringing waking her up. She looked at the name on the phone that read Lil Baby. She leaned over to try and pick it up, but he startled her when he picked up.

"I don't touch your phone, so don't ever fucking touch mine," Josh said through gritted teeth, and he climbed out of bed and called Chyna back. He walked towards the guest room, so that Iesha wouldn't hear the conversation.

"Hello," Chyna said into the phone.

"What's up? I saw that you called."

"Yeah, I was getting ready to go to sleep and wanted to see if you were feeling better."

"Yeah, I'm good, it was nice of you to think about me after you came home from your date." Josh was pissed that he'd allowed the words to come out his mouth. He couldn't even believe he was acting that way. He hated to admit it; when Iesha told him that Chyna was with another man, that made him feel some type of way.

"Okay, let's clear something up right now. We are not in a relationship, Josh. Nothing has changed between us. We are still just friends and not that it's any of your business, but I had dinner with my brother. I don't have to tell you what I am and not doing. I'm not questioning who or what you're doing in these streets. I will say this though, tell which ever one of your bitches that's watching me to mind they business or learn their facts first!" Chyna snapped into the phone before hanging up on him.

Josh looked down at his phone, shocked that Chyna had just snapped on him that way. It was funny though because he had literally just had the same exact conversation with Iesha. He knew that he was in the wrong and deserved that. He was happy to hear that she wasn't out with another man though. He sent her a text, apologizing than went to lay back down in bed. He made a mental note to go buy her something the following day to make it up to her.

"Josh," called out Iesha.

"Go to sleep, please," Josh said as he pulled her into his arms and went to sleep.

He could feel Iesha's tears falling onto his arm, but his migraine didn't allow the patience he needed to deal with her. If he felt better in the next couple of hours, he would give her some head and dick to get her his back off some.

❧ I I ❧

Chyna and Bri were chilling on the hood of Tim's BMW. He had invited Bri to come out to a party on one of his blocks, so of course, she dragged Chyna along with her. Typically, Chyna wouldn't attend events like that in the hood, but Bri had convinced her. Since she'd be starting school in a week, she'd enjoy one last event. Once school started, Chyna knew that she'd be extra busy, so she figured what the hell. Not only would she have her schoolwork, but she had a meeting set up with her plug in a couple of days, so she'd be busy hustling as well.

Chyna looked down at her phone and saw that she had a text from Maddox.

Mad: What's up, Chy, we just got in town and checked into our hotel. What you up to?

Me: I'm at a block party with my girl Bri, right now. What y'all about to do?

Mad: Matt and my pops about to go to see your parents, and I'm waiting on Rome. He's going to show me around a little bit.

Me: Okay cool, let me know when y'all done. We can probably hang out for a minute.

Mad: Alright, I'll hit your line later.

"Girl there's a nigga that's been eyeing you for the past five minutes, and he looks like he's about to come this way," Bri whispered, getting Chyna's attention.

Chyna looked up from her phone to see who Bri was referring to. She looked him and down then went back to her phone. There was no way she was even going to entertain him. He looked like he had been selling packs on the block all day. He had a nappy fro and dusty white ones; those were two negatives in her book. If he couldn't even keep his appearance up, there was no way she would go anywhere with him in public. Plus, she wasn't attracted to pack workers. The most he could do was join her team and work for her.

"What's up, lil mama, what's your name?"

"It's Chyna."

"Okay, I could make you my China doll. I'm Desmond, could I get your number? Maybe I could take you out sometime."

"Nah, I'm good," replied Chyna.

"Oh, I get it. You one of those stuck-up bitches."

Chyna looked at Desmond like he was crazy. She was trying to be nice, but he had asked for it.

"Nah nigga, I'm not stuck-up. I'm just a bitch that you can't afford, so get the fuck out of my face before I have somebody come beat your ass for disrespecting me," spat Chyna.

"Bitch, who you gone call? I'll wait for them!" Desmond yelled, walking closer to Chyna.

Chyna jumped up off the car and reached into her purse for her mace. She would mace the shit out him if he came any closer to her.

"Look, I'm not going to be too many more of your bitches and God is my witness, if you come any closer to me, your family gone be casket shopping soon for your bitch ass," threatened Chyna.

Desmond was about to respond when he felt somebody pull him by the collar.

"Yo, what the fuck are you doing up in her face like you about to do something? Since when you disrespect women?" Josh barked.

"Man, this bitch—" was all Desmond got out before Josh's fist connected with his jaw.

"Watch your fucking mouth. I literally just said we don't disrespect females like that."

"Yo, you tripping!" yelled Desmond.

"Lil nigga, you better go walk that shit off," Josh warned.

Desmond looked like he wanted to say something else, but Tim intervened.

"Aye, Des, just let it go. You can't run up on that man's girl and expect him not to say anything," Tim said as he pulled him away from the group.

"Damn, you out here looking all sexy and got nigga's ready to act crazy," Josh said as he lifted Chyna up and placed her back on the hood of the car, so he could stand between her legs.

Chyna had her long hair combed down straight and was rocking a Red Nike vintage romper with the black Prada purse and hat that her family bought her. She was also rocking some black Prada sneakers, courtesy of Josh. It was an apology gift to her for tripping on the phone the other day.

"Nah, these niggas just don't know how to take no for an answer. I'm not the one to play with. Had you not shown up when you did, I was about to mace his ass then call and have somebody come beat his ass."

"Look at you, all gangsta and shit," joked Josh.

"If you didn't know, now you know," replied Chyna.

"You smell good as hell," Josh complimented Chyna as he sucked on her neck.

"Thank you and don't start anything you can't finish," moaned Chyna.

"Come home with me tonight, and I'll show what I can finish. Hell, I'll even let you finish a few times before I do," smirked Josh.

"You know what, that's my cue to go. I'm about to go get something to drink, and I'll be back," Bri said, jumping down from the car.

"Is that so? I might just have to take you up on that offer. I have to drop something off, then I can meet you there afterwards, so you can finish me off," Chyna flirted.

"You already know I can take care of you. You got my dick jumping from the thought of it," Josh replied before sucking on Chyna's bottom lip then sticking his tongue down her throat, not caring that they were standing outside in public for everyone to see. She had him doing shit he typically wouldn't do in public, but he needed to show them nigga's that he fucked with her, so that they would know their place.

A couple of minutes later, Bri came over to Chyna in a hurry.

"Girl what's wrong with you?" Chyna asked, seeing the panic look on her friend face.

"I just saw your brother and some of his boys. He's down by Audrey's people house and he knows that you're here because he's standing by the car he got you."

Chyna let out a sigh before climbing down from the car.

"I'll be back in minute. Let me go see what he wants," Chyna said to Josh.

"Okay, I won't be far," replied Josh.

Chyna walked down to the middle of the block where Rome was standing with Maddox and his baby mama, Audrey

"What's up y'all," Chyna spoke to the group.

"Hey, Chyna," they all said simultaneously.

"You out here looking good," complimented Audrey.

"What are you doing out here?" Rome asked his sister.

"Bri was invited, and she asked me to come along with her."

"You know that you need to let me know when you're going to be in this area."

"Why? So, you can send one of your men to babysit me? I think not."

"You know it's not even about babysitting you. I got enemies out here that will try to get to you to get back at me. You know how this shit goes."

"I know, and I'll keep that in mind, but I plan on falling back from any of these blocks once I start school next week."

Rome was about to reply until he saw a group of girls walking near them, causing him to pull Chyna closer to him.

"Do you know them?" Rome asked Audrey.

Audrey looked in the direction that Rome was facing.

"One of the girls name is Iesha and one is Pam, but I don't know about the other ones. I just know those two because Pam lives down the street, and Iesha be around here a lot with her."

Chyna looked on as one of the bad body bitches pointed at her. She could already tell that they were on some bullshit, so she took her hat off and pulled her hair into a ponytail. She wanted to be ready in case one of them decided to run up on her.

"Hey, Audrey girl, I thought that was you," spoke Pam.

"What's up," Audrey replied back.

"So, who do we have here," Iesha said, looking Chyna up and down.

"Man, y'all can go on somewhere with that bullshit because whatever y'all think is about to happen, is not even about to go down like that," Rome interjected.

"You don't have to worry about anything happening to the little hoe. I just wanted to warn her to stop fucking with Josh because he belongs to me."

Chyna instantly burst into laughter from Iesha's words. She couldn't believe the bitch was approaching her over him.

"Baby girl, if that nigga belonged to you, there would be no need for you to be approaching my sister. Just go back to wherever you came from, and we'll act like this never happened," said Rome.

"Bitch, you got to be dumb as fuck to even come over here and approach me about him. Y'all hoes out here looking bad behind these niggas. You and your little crew can get the fuck out of my face though."

"Oh, you bad cause your brother standing here. What you gone do if I don't?" questioned Iesha.

Chyna pulled her phone from her pocket and dialed Josh's number.

"What's up, baby?" Josh asked on the first ring.

"You got about thirty seconds to come down this street and talk some sense into your bitch or you gone be helping her ass up off this ground when I finish with her," Chyna warned before hanging up the phone.

"Bitch, you not gone do shit!" Iesha yelled.

Chyna took her purse off and handed it to Audrey.

"Don't say I didn't try to warn you," Rome smirked. He had taught his sister how to fight, so he was confident that she was going to win.

"Okay, let me make it clear to you why you about to get this ass whooping. I'm not fighting you over Josh. I'm about to fuck you up off the principle of you coming in my face trying to play me like I'm some weak bitch, and I might just go to his house and let him eat my pussy once I'm finished!" Chyna exclaimed before stepping forward and knocking Iesha in the mouth.

Iesha attempted to grab Chyna, but Chyna hit her with another right hook followed by a left. She tried to keep up, but Chyna's hands were too fast for her. Chyna grabbed a handful of Iesha's weave and proceeded to beat the fuck out of her. Iesha continued to grab at Chyna to try and stop her, but it wasn't happening. By then, a crowd had surrounded them and all you heard were ooh's and ahh's from everybody.

One of the girls looked like they were about to try and jump in, but Rome lifted up the front of his shirt, showing his piece and causing her and her other friends to take few steps back.

"Damn, Esh, you getting your ass fucked up. How you from the projects and can't fight!" one of the guys yelled out, causing some of the people to laugh.

"Bitch, did you have enough yet?" Chyna asked as she landed a punch on Iesha's shoulder blade.

"Yo, what the fuck is going on here!" Josh yelled, grabbing at Chyna.

"Don't fucking grab my sister. Your girl asked for this ass whooping the minute she came in Chyna's face. It'll teach her about overstepping boundaries!" snapped Rome.

Josh's attempt to grab Chyna threw her off and allowed Iesha to get the upper hand. Iesha grabbed Chyna's arm and threw her to the ground. She was about to try and kick her, but Chyna sat up and grabbed Iesha's leg midair, pulling her to the ground and causing her to hit her head hard on the concrete.

Chyna jumped up from the ground just in case Iesha tried something, but she could see that she wasn't because she could barely stand. One of her friends helped her up from the ground and started walking her towards her home. Once she knew everything was good, she turned her attention to Josh.

"I told your ass to keep shit one hundred with me. If you had a bitch, you should have told me from the beginning when you were begging to eat my pussy. I didn't fight her because of you, though, because I don't fight over niggas, and I'm damn sure not fighting over one that's not mine. I beat her ass because she needs to learn that when someone says get the fuck out of their face that's what they mean."

"That's not my girlfriend, Chyna. She's my ex-girlfriend."

"You don't have to convince me, Josh. I don't give a fuck if she's your woman or ex. Make sure she stays out of my business and out of my face," warned Chyna.

"I'll have a talk with her, but are you still coming over tonight?" Josh asked, causing Chyna to laugh.

"Nah, playboy, I'm going home tonight. You gone have to work hard to even get me to go out on another date with your ass, and it's going to take a lot more than a pair of Prada shoes this time," smirked Chyna.

"Josh, you ain't shit. I don't even know why Iesha wants your ass back!" one of Iesha's friends spat as she walked away.

Josh ignored the girl and kept his attention on Chyna. "Can you at least text me when you get home?" Josh asked.

"I'll think about," Chyna replied before turning her attention towards her brother.

"Damn girl, I'm going to have to call you Baby Ali," joked Maddox.

"Shut up," replied Chyna.

"You good, baby girl?" Rome asked as he examined his sister.

"Yeah, I'm good. I'm about to head home though.

"Can you do me a favor and save me a trip by taking Mad with you? I was supposed to take him back to the house, so that he could leave with his father and brother, but we need to go pick up the kids from her mom's house."

"Okay, that's fine. I'll text you when I make it home," replied Chyna.

"You about to go?" Bri asked as she approached Chyna.

"Yeah, I'm about to call it a night since I'm not going to Josh's house. His ass about to have to sweat for a minute."

"I know that's right; from what I heard, Iesha got hands. She just wasn't a match for you."

"Well, I hope it was a lesson for any other bitch that thinks they can try me."

"They let that innocent baby face fool them but hit my line tomorrow and let me know what you on. I'm about to stick around with Tim a little longer."

"Alright, babes," Chyna responded before heading to the silver BMW Rome let her keep.

Chyna climbed into the car with Maddox right behind her. She connected her phone to the radio and allowed the music to play. Neither Chyna nor Maddox said anything during the ride. Chyna hated that Maddox had seen that side of her; it was like she was having a meltdown both times he'd seen her. She could tell that he wanted to say something but was refraining from saying it.

Once they pulled up to her house, she parked the car in the garage and climbed out. She was about to walk through the door when Maddox pulled her arm and pushed her up against the car.

"You're too beautiful to be out here fighting. Leave that hood rat shit for the birds. If that nigga can't make up his mind about what he want to do, then it's time to let somebody else show you how you should be treated."

"Let me guess, you're that somebody else, Maddox? What makes you so different?"

"Only time will tell, sweetheart, but I'm far from a fuck nigga," Maddox smirked before kissing her on the forehead, causing her to blush.

Chyna and Maddox walked through the kitchen door where they found their parents sitting in the living room.

"Hey, everybody," Chyna spoke before hugging her Uncle Marcel.

"I'm surprised you're home so early on a Friday night. It's only 10:30," said Chyna's father.

"Yeah, I had other plans, but they got canceled, so I decided to come home since Rome needed to go pick up the kids. He didn't want to have to double back."

"Marcel and I are going to take care of some business, tomorrow, while he's out here and then we're going to go to one of the bars afterwards. I was hoping you'd cancel whatever you had planned tomorrow, so that you could help Matteo get settled in and then maybe show them around a little. You could probably take them to Navy Pier or something. I'll give you some money," replied Mr. Black.

"Okay, that won't be a problem. But I'm about to go to bed now, so I'll see y'all tomorrow," Chyna replied before heading upstairs.

"Well, that was easier than I thought. She must be up to something," said Mr. Black.

"Leave the girl alone. Maybe she just has something going on. Be happy that she's cooperating," replied Mrs. Black.

Chyna went into her room and grabbed and grabbed a t-shirt then went to the bathroom to take a shower. Once her shower was finished, she climbed into bed and went straight to sleep.

❧ 12 ❧

The following morning, Chyna woke up to the sounds of people walking back and forth. It was already eleven; she couldn't believe she had just slept for twelve hours. Her body was more tired than she'd realized. She climbed out of bed and put on a pair of shorts and went into the hall to see what was going on.

"Good morning, sleeping beauty," spoke Matteo.

"Good morning, how long have y'all been here?"

"We just got here about fifteen minutes ago."

"Okay, just let me get cleaned up, and I can help y'all."

"You don't have to help us carry boxes. Your brother-in-law is helping out since your sister is visiting."

Chyna rolled her eyes; she hoped that Chloe didn't say anything to piss her off.

"Hey, Chy," spoke Nate.

"What's going on," Chyna said as she walked towards the bathroom to take care of her personal hygiene. Once she finished, she walked downstairs where Maddox was walking in and carrying a box.

"Hey, Maddox."

"Hey, Chyna. What time did you want to leave? I was

thinking of leaving my truck here, and we can go wherever you had planned, in your car. That way my dad would have a way back."

"That's fine, we can leave whenever y'all done. I'm about to grab something to eat and clean up my room before getting dressed."

"Okay, cool," Maddox replied before walking up the stairs with the box.

"Hey, y'all," Chyna greeted the Chloe and her mom.

"Hey, Chy," they both said in unison.

"There's breakfast sitting in the microwave for you," said Mrs. Black.

"Thanks, ma," Chyna replied before putting the microwave on a minute. She took the plate from the microwave then grabbed some silverware and sat at the counter. Her mom had made some eggs, breakfast potatoes, turkey bacon, and biscuits. Chyna hadn't eaten since early the following evening, so she felt like she was starving.

"So, when are you going to introduce everyone to your new boyfriend?" Chloe asked, catching Chyna off guard.

"What boyfriend?" Chyna questioned.

"The one that you been seen around the city with. One of Nathan's cousins said she be seeing you with him and that he stands on the corner and sales drugs."

"Okay, let me stop you right there. Tell Nathan's cousin to stay out of my business. I don't have a boyfriend. He's just a friend, and he doesn't stand on corners. You would never even catch me entertaining someone that stands on a corner. My standards are way higher than that."

"Yeah, but not so high that you have to deal with a criminal."

"Do you hear yourself, right now? What is half the men in this family? How do you think you even have a job? That company was bought by a criminal and dirty money. Don't put your foot in your mouth just because you want to look down on me."

"Aye, that's enough, you two. Chloe, leave your sister alone and let her eat her food," said Mrs. Black.

Chyna was glad that Chloe brought up Josh in front of her mother and not her father. Her mother was actually the lenient parent. It was her father that was the overprotective one. The only issue with her mother was that she became mute whenever Chyna's father was around.

Chyna finished her breakfast then headed upstairs to clean up her bedroom. Once she finished cleaning, she went to the bedroom that Matteo would be staying in a couple doors down and checked in on them. They were almost finished bringing everything up, so Chyna started helping them put stuff away. By the time they were finished, it was almost two thirty, so Chyna allowed them to finish while she went to get ready.

Chyna took a shower then combed her hair into a bun. She looked in the closet and put on a pair of blue jean shorts with a white half-shirt and a pair of white Prada sneakers. She applied some lip gloss then grabbed her white Prada purse and phone from the nightstand before exiting the room. Chyna looked down at her phone and saw that she had a missed call from Josh. She didn't bother about calling him back. She'd call him later when she wasn't busy. Chyna walked down the stairs and found everybody sitting in the living room.

"I'm about to go now, ma, if you need me, call. I'll be back tonight," said Chyna.

"Okay, y'all be careful out there," replied Mrs. Black.

Chyna headed to the car, and Maddox got in the front seat while Matteo got in the back. She jumped on the expressway and took the thirty five-minute drive to downtown then parked in Navy Pier parking garage.

"Have y'all ever been here before?" asked Chyna.

"When we were younger," replied Matteo.

"Okay, we can walk around and get on some of the rides," suggested Chyna.

The group walked around for a bit then took a speed boat

tour, which was actually fun for everyone. After that, Chyna convinced them to get on the Light Tower and the Centennial Wheel. She stopped at Build-A-Bear to get bears for both her niece and nephew. She knew they both would love it.

"Okay, we've been out her for hours, can we go somewhere to eat, now?" asked Matteo.

"Yeah, we can go to Grand Lux Café, it's one of my favorite restaurants down here," replied Chyna.

Chyna and the guys left Navy Pier and climbed in her car then headed towards the restaurant. She gave her keys to the valet driver, and after waiting twenty minutes, the hostess showed them to their seats. The waiter immediately came and took their orders and was gone as fast as she came.

"Are you ready to start school?" asked Maddox.

"Yeah, I am. I'm still kind of mad about not moving out right now, but it is what it is. If things go as I have planned, I'll be in my own crib by this time next year. I refuse to live with my parents longer than a year. I can't even have company unless it's Bri, and I'm not on that. Rome suggested I moved in with him, but that's not any better than staying with my parents. Well, technically, I guess it is since Rome be out a lot, but I'm not that cruel to leave Matteo to get back and forth with my parents."

"Good looking out, Chyna, but it should only be about six or seven months. Once Maddox moves out here for good, I'll be moving in with him and have my own car."

"I know, I'm not tripping about it. I got somethings lined up for me, so I'm good. Did you decide where you want to find a house at?"

"Not yet, I've been looking though. Do you have any suggestions?"

"If you want to be close to the school, I suggest Hyde Park. It's a good area, and they have nice condos and townhouses since it's just you and Matteo. Now, if you want something big and nice, you can try Olympia Fields where we at or Orland Park. That's where Rome lives."

"What about your sister? She doesn't live in a good area?" asked Matteo.

"Yeah, she does, but I wouldn't suggest it for y'all. She and her husband have a condo in one of the high-rise buildings about five minutes from here. It's congested all the time with traffic, and you have to pay for parking. Plus, there's so many rules for those apartments."

Chyna continued to talk with Matteo and Maddox over dinner. Once they finished dinner, Chyna was about to pay since her father had given her money. Maddox had paid for everything at the pier, but he stopped her and paid that bill as well.

"So, what do y'all want to do for the rest of the rest of the night?" asked Chyna.

"Can you take me back to the hotel, so that I can get some sleep? I've only had about eight hours combined for the past three days. I want to be rested, so by time Monday come, I'll be ready for school."

"Sure, I can take you to the hotel," said Chyna.

"How about you stop at a liquor store first, then we can just kick it in my room," suggested Maddox.

Chyna drove to Binny's Beverage Depot where Maddox inside and grabbed a fifth of Patron before heading to his hotel. They climbed onto the elevator and took it to the top floor to the Executive King Suite.

"Goodnight, see y'all tomorrow," said Matteo.

"Goodnight," Chyna and Maddox replied in unison.

Chyna and Maddox entered the room, and Chyna chuckled at the irony. Maddox was staying in the exact same kind of suite that Chyna and Josh stayed in while in Memphis.

"You can take your shoes off and get comfortable. I got a small Bluetooth speaker over on the table, so you can connect your phone to it and play some music if you like. I'm about to use the bathroom then grab some glasses," Maddox suggested.

Chyna took her shoes off and sat on the couch, then hooked

her phone up to the speaker. She turned on Pandora R&B station. By time the music started playing, Maddox came walking towards her in a tank top and shorts. Her eyes immediately glanced down at his print. She hurriedly lifted her eyes before he caught her staring.

Chyna and Maddox talked and played a drinking game until both of them were tipsy. They didn't know if it had to do with the liquor or the built-up sexual tension from all the flirting, but one thing led to another, and Chyna was straddling his lap while he was pulling down the top part of her jumpsuit.

Maddox ran his index finger across Chyna's lips before kissing them softly, then made his way to her neck and breasts. A soft moan escaped her lips as he took his time, sucking on both of her breast. He stood her up from the couch and pulled her jumpsuit and underwear all the way down before picking her up and leading her to his bedroom. He laid down on the bed and pulled her on top of him, so that they could be in the sixty-nine position. She had never given head a day in her life, but she did watch porn and take a fellatio class after she first had sex with Josh, so that she could learn some pointers on how to please him, but it looked like she would be showing her skills off to Maddox.

Chyna sucked and hummed on his balls before taking him into her mouth. She could tell from the intensity of how he was eating her out that she must have been doing something right. He was sucking on her pussy so good, she was losing concertation. He lifted her leg up, so she could straddle his face and ride it how she wanted. She held on to the headboard and rode Maddox's mouth until she was squirting in it. She tried to get up, but he held her thighs tighter and continued to suck until she was cumming again.

Maddox finally released Chyna's trembling leg and leaned over and grabbed the magnum from his nightstand. He had already planned on having sex with Chyna since the night before. He saw the way she looked at him; the same way he looked at her. They both lusted over each other, so there was no point in denying it.

Maddox slid the condom on, and Chyna wasted no time sliding down on his dick, causing both of them to moan. She moved up and down then around slowly as she held onto the headboard.

"Fuck, you feel so fucking good," Maddox groaned as he bit into her shoulder blade.

He couldn't even hide his excitement if he wanted to. It felt like he had died and gone to heaven. He could see why Josh was acting crazy and sweating her now. She had the kind of pussy that had you ready to pay all her bills just to hit it.

"Yesssss, you do too, baby," Chyna moaned as she picked up the pace, but Maddox slowed her down and held onto her waste.

"Nah, ma, we about to have to switch places because at the rate you going, you about to turn me into a minute man," Maddox said seriously as he flipped Chyna onto her back then slid deep inside of her. He lifted one of her legs into the crook of his leg and proceeded to give her the dick nice and slow. She had good pussy, but he had to show her that he could still tame the shit.

"Oh, my God. Maddox, you about to make me cum."

"Nah, hold that shit, I don't want you to come yet. If you come right now, I'm going to stop," threatened Maddox.

Chyna clenched her pussy tighter around his dick to keep her body from coming until he picked up the pace and told her that she could cum now. Her body started shaking, and she was squirting all over his dick.

Maddox flipped her over to the side of the bed and entered her from behind. He grabbed a hold of her ponytail and fucked her hard. Having sex with him was definitely different from when she slept with Josh. She didn't know if it was because Josh was taking his time since it was her first time or if Maddox was more passionate about his sex game. Either way it went, she was loving every bit of what he was doing to her. They went at it for about forty-five minutes before they both were coming together, but they picked up round two in the bathroom then back in the bed. They went at it off and on for three hours until they both were in the bed, unable to move. Chyna didn't care that it was one in the morning. There was no way in hell she was going to get up and try to drive home. Between the Patron and sex, it was over with. She'd deal with the consequences later.

"Maddox," Chyna called out as she snuggled up against him.

"Yes?" asked Maddox.

"Can we keep this between us and not let it make our friendship weird?"

"Yeah, I can keep it between us and the only way our friendship will get weird is if you allow it. I'm leaving to go back home tomorrow night, anyway, but I would like for you to have lunch with me tomorrow. I don't want you to think that I just used you for sex."

"I wouldn't think that. I'm young but not naïve. I knew that you were going back home tomorrow. We did something that we both wanted to do from the first time we saw each other, and I'm fine with that. You can go home and finish taking care of your business, and I'll stay here and take care of mine. Once you come back out here for good, we can work on our friendship," suggested Chyna.

"Okay, I like that, but remember, I'm always here to talk. Even if it's about that fuck nigga. You can talk to me about him."

"He's not that bad," laughed Chyna.

Chyna and Maddox talked for about thirty minutes until they both were exhausted and ready to pass out.

The following day, Chyna woke up to Maddox rubbing on her clit. She opened her legs a little wider, so he could get to it better. Once he felt that she was nice and wet, he slid inside of her from the side, causing a moan to escape both of their mouths. He had woken up with his shit on brick and her ass rubbing up against it. He couldn't resist hitting it one more time before he left. He already knew it was going to be a problem once he moved to Chicago because it was going to be hard to resist her.

Maddox figured out that she was trouble the first time he laid eyes on her. She was meant to date his brother, but she had let it be known that he wouldn't have been able to tame her, and he knew that she was right. His brother was a good boy. Hell, he hadn't even had sex yet. Meanwhile, Chyna was the woman that they warned you about; she was only eighteen and already a beast. He could only imagine how'd she'd be once she was older.

Maddox and Chyna had sex for about thirty minutes until he was cumming. They got up to take a shower when there was a knock at his door.

"Shit," he said as he stood up from the bed and slipped on his boxers, "wait right here, let me go see who that is," said Maddox.

Maddox walked to the door and looked through the peephole and saw that it was his brother. He opened the door halfway to see what he wanted.

"Hey, I was trying to see if you wanted to go down and grab some breakfast before y'all drop me off."

"Okay, just let me throw on some clothes right quick," replied Maddox.

"Alright, I can just come in and wait then we can go down together," Matteo suggested as he pushed past his brother.

Matteo walked over to the couch, and his eyes immediately fell on Chyna's clothes. He shook his head as he looked up at his brother.

Maddox ignored his brother's look as he picked up Chyna clothes and took them in the bathroom.

"Come on, let's take a shower," Maddox said as he led into the bathroom. He turned the water on hot then they both climbed in. He caressed the side of her face then kissed her gently on the lips.

"He knows I'm here, doesn't he?"

"Yeah, he saw your clothes on the floor, but he won't say anything to anyone about it."

"Okay, I hope not," Chyna replied as they finished showering.

"I got this covered, just relax," Maddox said, trying to reassure her.

Chyna grabbed the clothes that she had on the night before and put them on except for the underwear; she stuck those inside of her purse. She grabbed a brush that Maddox had on the dresser and combed her hair, so that the sex wouldn't be obvious. Once she was satisfied with her appearance, she joined Maddox and Matteo in the living room.

"Hey, Matteo," spoke Chyna.

"Hey, Chyna," Matteo responded back.

"Look, I'm not sure what Maddox told you, but I kind of need two favors."

"What are the favors?"

"I need you to keep me staying here with Maddox between us. My parents are already strict as it is with me, and I'm really not trying to mess up things with Maddox and my family. I know I'm younger than him and that we were drinking last night, but he didn't take advantage of me, and it wasn't the liquor. I would have slept with him rather I was sober or not. The other favor is, I need you to cover for me. I need you to say we were hanging out late, and I spent the night with you."

"What?" they both asked in unison.

"I'm not asking you to say that we slept together or nothing like that. I'm about to call my brother and ask him to cover for me with my parents. I know once I ask him, he's going to ask questions, so I have to tell him that I was here. The thing is if I tell him that I spent the night with Maddox, he's going to know I slept with him. While if I tell him that I fell asleep on your couch, it would be more convincing. My parent's act like they don't know my type, but Rome does. He knows that I would mess with somebody older than me from the streets as opposed to a college student my age. I'm begging you, I'll make it up to you," pleaded Chyna.

"Alright, I hope you know what you're doing," warned Matteo.

"I do, thank you so much. I just need to call my brother, then I'll sneak out before y'all father see me."

Chyna picked her phone up from the table and saw that she had two missed calls from her mother and one from Rome. She took a deep breath before dialing Rome's number.

"Hello," Rome answered.

"Hello," replied Chyna.

"What the fuck, Chyna? Are you alright? Pops called me saying you didn't come home last night. I know you didn't go and spend the night with that nigga after the stunt he pulled."

"No, Rome, I haven't even talked to him since that night. I need you to cover for me and tell pops that I spent the night at your house."

"How am I supposed to do that when he called me earlier, and I told him that you weren't with me?"

"Just tell him that you can in early this morning and that I'd been sleep when you got there, so you didn't realize I was there. Please Rome, I just need you to do this for me. I'm not trying to have another fight with dad right now," Chyna pleaded.

"Okay, I'm going to do it, but you need to tell me where you are. Are you in some kind of trouble or something? You know, I'll come to you."

"No, it's not anything like that. I went out yesterday with Maddox and Matteo. We ended up going to the liquor store, and I had a little too much to drink. I wasn't comfortable enough to drive home, so I ended up falling asleep on Matteo's couch, and by time, I woke up it was morning."

"Now, this isn't just an excuse because you stayed with Josh?"

"No, Rome, when I stay with Josh, I use Bri as a cover up. I'm not talking to him right now, so that's not even an option. I can let you hear Matteo if that'll make you more comfortable," said Chyna.

The other end of the line was silent, so Chyna could tell that he was contemplating finding out if she was lying or not.

Chyna put the phone by Matteo, so he could say something.

"Hey, Rome, she's telling the truth. She's been here all night," stated Matteo.

"Are you happy, now?" Chyna asked.

"Alright, Chyna, I'll call pops and tell him that you just left my house and should be heading home now, but you better hurry up and get there. I'll be stopping by the house later on."

"Okay, thank you so much. I told Bri I'd meet up with her at three, but I should be back home by seven."

"Alright, text me when you get home. Love you," said Rome.

"I love you too," Chyna replied before hanging up.

Chyna turned around and saw Matteo and Maddox, staring at her in disbelief.

"I don't know if you being able to lie so smoothly is good or bad thing," chuckled Maddox.

"It was just a little white lie. I just lied about who bed I slept in and omitted the part about having sex," smirked Chyna.

"Matt, go try to stall pops from leaving out while I walk her down the stairs," said Maddox.

"Okay, I'll see you later, Chyna."

"See you, Matt," Chyna replied as she grabbed her things before, she and Maddox headed to her car.

"We're going to come by y'all house around seven and stay for a few hours. My pops don't want to get on the road until about eleven, so that way we won't have to deal with any traffic, so I'll see you then."

"Alright, I'll be home by then."

Maddox kissed Chyna on the forehead before she climbed in the car and headed home. Chyna pulled up to her house and parked in the driveway. She saw that the living room was empty and ran up to her bedroom. She thought she had avoided her parents, but it seemed she wasn't that lucky.

"Chyna," Mrs. Black called out.

"Yes, Ma," replied Chyna.

"Can you come down here, so that we can talk?"

"Okay, can I at least change my clothes real quick?"

"Yeah," responded Mrs. Black.

Chyna went into her bedroom and took the clothes off from the night before. She pulled out a pair of red underwear and put them on along with a pair of black shorts and an orange crop top. She grabbed her orange Pink slides and put them on, then headed down the stairs to speak with her mother.

Mrs. Black lectured Chyna for almost twenty minutes about how important is to check-in and how much she and her father were worried about her and that if she was going to stay at Rome's house, she needed to let them know ahead of time. Chyna sat through it quietly and agreed to everything that her mother had said because it could have been worse. She could have been getting lectured from her father.

Chyna looked at the time and ran upstairs to switch the contents of her purse then headed to the spot where she was meeting Bri's brother, Byron. She looked around and made sure that everything was straight before sending him a text message, letting him know she was outside. She sat in the car and waited until he opened the door before climbing out and going to meet him.

"Damn, lil Chy, you not so little no more," Byron said, looking her up and down.

"Yeah, I been eating my Wheaties," Chyna flirted back.

Chyna walked into the empty house with Byron and followed him into the kitchen.

"So, Bri says that you needed to talk to me about some business. What did you have in mind?"

"I just need you to get me in touch with your plug, and I'll take care of the rest. I want pills and weed only. Y'all can keep the dope and all that other shit."

"You do know your family got they own connect and could probably get you a way better deal? Hell, I been trying to get up with they connect."

"Yeah, I know, and I went to my brother, but he turned me down."

"So, what do I get for helping you? This is a huge risk I'm taking; I don't want any problems with Rome or your peoples."

"Come on now, Byron. I would never throw you under the bus. Your name won't even come up in any of this, if Rome asks. Name your price or percentage, and I got you."

"I don't want your money, baby girl. Just give me one night with you, and I got you. We can even keep it between us."

Chyna sat back in the seat and thought about it for a minute. In order to do what she wanted, she needed Byron for more than just his plug.

"Okay, let's make a deal. If you want to hit this, I'm going to need more than just your plug. My shit is A1, and you won't be disappointed."

"Alright, what did you have in mind?"

"I need you to set me up a meeting with a few bad bitches that's about their money. Preferably a stripper and one that's a scammer or hustle niggas for me. You get me that and a meeting with your plug, and you can get two hours of my time."

Byron nodded his head up at down at Chyna's negotiating skills. "Bet, I got you. Get me one week, and I'll have everything in place for you. You just be ready to keep your end of the deal."

"Don't worry about me keeping my end. You just better make sure you make the two hours count because that's the only chance you getting. I'm not about to make it a habit of fucking my brother's best friend," Chyna said, standing from the seat and heading towards the door. Her business was finished, so there was no need for her to stay there.

"I'll text you once everything is straight with a time, date, and location."

"Alright, just make sure it's in the evening time if it's during the week. I start school tomorrow."

Chyna walked to her car and climbed in, then headed home. She just hoped Byron kept his end of the deal because if he did, it would be just the break she needed to have enough money to leave home comfortably. She technically had enough money in her bank account to live off of for a year, but then after that year, she'd be back at square one because she didn't want to work at anybody's job. she wouldn't be able to keep up with the lifestyle she lived at the age of eighteen with a regular job. She wanted to be able leave home and still have the same lifestyle her father provided her, and she already knew if she left home and didn't work for the family business, he would cut her off and wanted to be prepared.

❧ 14 ❧

Chyna was sitting at her desk in her bedroom, studying when a text message came through her phone. She looked down at her phone and saw that Byron had texted, saying his plug and girls agreed to meet up with her. She was happy to see that message; she had been going to school and studying all week, waiting for that moment. She replied back to it and went back to her books for about another hour. Once she finished her homework, she went and took a quick shower, then went back to her room to get dressed. She had never met him before, so he set it up for him to meet her downtown at The Westin. Since she had to meet up with the women Byron picked her, she needed something to wear that fit both occasions.

Chyna put on a pair of black jeggings, a black lace bra, and a black boyfriend one-button blazer with a pair of black Christian Louboutin heels. She put her silver Rolex on and cross chain then combed her long hair down. She applied a light coat of make-up and her MAC lip gloss. She packed her overnight bag then grabbed her phone and purse from the table. She stopped in Matteo's room before leaving since he was the only one at home.

"Hey, Matt, I'm about to go. If my parents come in and ask, just let them know I left already and that I'll be back tomorrow."

"Okay, be careful," replied Matteo.

Over the past week, Chyna and Matteo had been getting along well. He was actually the first guy friend, she had that didn't want to have sex with her.

Chyna hopped in her car and headed downtown to The Westin hotel. She parked her car and got out and checked in. She left a note at the front desk to give the plug when he made it there.

Chyna walked inside of her suite and put her bag in the closet. Since she had both meetings and her night with Byron, she was staying in the room that night. He had already booked a room of his own that she was going to go to when she was ready. She was seriously about him only getting two hours, so once she was done, she was heading back up to her own room.

Chyna was just about to sit down when there was a light knock at the door. She got up and walked to the door and opened it for the handsome stranger. He was tall with a light brown complexion and drugs. He had a slight rough around the edge look to him.

"Hey, beautiful, you must be Chyna," he said, extending his hand.

"I am, but what is your name?"

"You can call me Mase, I hope you don't mind, but I brought one of my men with me."

"Actually, I do. No offense, but I'm not comfortable sitting in a hotel room with two strangers. He's free to look around the room and I can show you that I'm not wearing a wire, so that you'll know I'm not setting you up. He can even hold onto my cellphone. I'd be more comfortable if he waited in the hallway during the meeting though," said Chyna.

Mase smirked at Chyna's comment.

"I like you already," he said to Chyna and nodded his head at the guy with him, giving him the okay to look around.

Chyna and Mase stood quietly, looking at each other for almost ten minutes while waiting on him to finish his sweep.

"It's all clear. I can search her now," said the guy.

"Nah, it doesn't work like that. It's going to cost you to touch me. I can show you I'm wire free on my own."

Chyna took her blazer jacket off, showing nothing but her bra then she pulled her pants down and turned around, so that they could see that nothing was there either. Both men were still staring as she pulled her pants back up. She didn't bother about putting the jacket back on.

"Alright, Trav, she's good, you can go now."

"Not so fast, it's your turn," Chyna nodded at Mase.

Mase lifted his black V-neck shirt up and then pulled down his jeans.

"Do you want me to pull the boxers down? That's when I'll have to charge you though," he smirked.

"Nah, you good," Chyna replied as she sat at the table.

Mase sat at the table with Chyna while Trav stepped out of the room.

"So, let's get down to business. B tells me that you need pills and weed. Are you looking for a front or something?"

"No, I just need you to tell me how much for each quantity I want, and I'll give you the cash. No fronting or loaning. Just straight business transitions per product."

"You're kind of young. Are you trying to put a nigga you fuck with, on or something?"

Chyna let out a slight chuckle at the sound of that.

"Look, I don't mean to sound cocky or anything but if I got to put a nigga on, the only thing I could do is add him to my payroll. I'm doing this for myself, which is why I said pills and weed only. I have a method that I'm going to do to make shit happen. This doesn't have anything to do with a man. This is about me making my own. The only thing I need you to do is get me the product, and you'll get your money in full. Once I get rid of what I got from you, then I'll order more."

"Okay let's talk numbers," said Mase.

Chyna and Mase sat and discussed numbers and a more common meet up place for them. They both agreed to meet in another week. She would bring the money, and he'd bring the product. Once the meeting was done, she only had five minutes left before the girls that she was meeting with started showing up.

Chyna reached in her bag and took out the bottle of Tequila that she had some guy pick up for her from the store. She threw back two shots before there was knock at her door. Three women came walking into the room; all three of them were beautiful, but one of them stood out too much for her. She could already tell that she wasn't going to work with her because she brought unnecessary attention from the green hair alone. Now, the other two looked like something she could work with. She just had to talk to them, first, to see where their heads were to determine if she'd work with them or not. She needed females on her team with the same drive as her.

"So, Yakea, tell me why you're a good fit to join my team? I mean, you're beautiful, but it takes more than looks to make it."

"It's like this, I'm about my paper by any means necessary. I work at Ocean Gentlemen's Club Friday through Sunday, and I do personal events. I grew up on the low end, so I'm connected with some street niggas. Speaking of niggas, I use what I got to get what I want from them. I'm not going to lie, I fuck some of them sometimes, but I get every single one of my bills paid without having to touch my own money. With everything that I have going on, I can get the clientele and be discreet with it. I'm persuasive and a good salesperson," said Yakea.

"Okay, and what can you bring to the team, Robin?" asked Chyna.

"Well, I crack cards, and I'm a booster. I also fuck around with some boss niggas for money. I don't set niggas up or no shit like that though. I live out West, and I'm just trying to stack my paper, so that me and my three-year-old son can move out of my grandmother's crib," replied Robin.

"Alright, and lastly, Tess. What's your special skill?"

"I dance and fuck with street niggas. I'm basically a runner and lookout. I pick up and drop off products. I don't have a sad story or anything like that. I'm just a young bitch out here trying to live the life I deserve," responded Tess.

"I'm not gone lie; I like all three of you, and I can find a place for each of your skills, but I have a few rules. I also want you to know what it is that I'm about to do and what y'all will be getting into. Once I finish, if you down, we'll set up another meeting with the other part of my team. If not, there's no hard feelings. Okay?"

"Okay," all three women said in unison.

"First to start off, from the bat, none of you would be doing anything that would get you real time if you ever got caught. If you do exactly what I tell you, you shouldn't ever have that problem. If it does occur that you get locked up, I have someone on payroll for you to contact, and they'll bond you out. I'm not fucking with coke, rocks, blows, or any of those other jobs. I'm strictly dealing with pills and weed only as far as drugs. In about six months, I want to open a shop or store as a front. So, that's where the boosting and card cracking would come in handy. I'll give you a place to sale your merchandise, and I'll keep a percentage of that. I'll also buy shit off of you and sell it. I'm not allowing anybody to know what's going in the next person's pocket. Once I choose to work with you and tell you the product you got to run, I'll tell you the percentage of what you'll make. How does that sound, so far?"

"Where do you sign me up at?" asked Yakea.

"Right, a bitch need to get put on to this," said Robin.

"It sounds like a plan, but what are you rules?" inquired Tess.

"None of you are allowed to discuss that you work for me. If somebody asks you questions tell them to mind their business, and if that isn't enough, tell them you can set up a meeting with me. Hair colors can't be super bright; we need to be able to keep a low profile. Shit like that is a target. I'm not saying you have to stick with black but not bright colors. That's the easiest way to pick you out of a line up. You can be ratchet and do whatever you want whenever you want as long as you not pushing my product at that time. All three of you have bodies, but I need to make sure that you're in shape, so you'll have to work out with me at least two days out of a week. Do you have any questions?"

"No," all three women said.

"Okay, I don't want an answer tonight. I want y'all to go home and think about it for the next two days. Text me Monday by seven p.m. the words *when are we going to the gym?* If you text that then I know you're in, and I'll send the next instructions. If not, then it was nice meeting you," Chyna replied as she stood from the seat.

Chyna walked all three girls out, then looked down at her phone and saw that Byron had texted his room number, which was only one floor under her. She replied back and told him she'd be down in five minutes. She took a deep breath to mentally prepare herself for what she was about to do. She couldn't believe that she was about to have sex with somebody that she had absolutely no feelings for. She didn't even lust over him, but a deal was a deal. He put her on like he said he would, so now it was her time to keep her end of the deal.

Chyna looked in her overnight bag and put on her tank top then headed out the door. When she made it down to Byron's room, his door was already cracked. She walked into his room and found him sitting on the bed in nothing but his boxers. She knew what she was there for, so she stripped off all her clothes to get right to the point.

Byron pulled her close to him and tried to kiss her on the lips, but she turned her head and allowed him to kiss her neck instead.

"You're so fucking beautiful," Byron whispered as he slowly

sucked on her neck and rubbed on her clit. Once he felt her getting moist, he laid her on the bed and stuck his head between her legs and started sucking on her clit, but it felt more like he was biting. He was down there for almost ten minutes, and she still hadn't cum, so she had to fake it.

"Oh my God, Byron, I'm about to come, baby. Hurry up and let me come on that dick!" screamed Chyna.

Chyna figured he must've bought it because he climbed from in between her legs, dropped his boxers, and reached over to grab a trojan condom from the nightstand. She raised up on her elbows to make sure he was actually putting the condom on and couldn't believe her eyes. His dick was nowhere near as big or Maddox or Josh's. The nigga dick was skinny and short. She laid back and closed her eyes, awaiting what was about to happen next.

Byron grunted and then started moving back and forth. The crazy part was Chyna hadn't even felt him slide all the way in.

"Damn, girl, you got some good pussy. I'm about to tear this shit up," Byron groaned.

"Yeah, baby, just like that. Make me cum for you, baby!" Chyna yelled out, faking an orgasm.

Byron was pumping for about another minute then stopped moving and started breathing heavy.

What the fuck was that Chyna thought to herself.

"Shit, Chy, your shit was good as hell. You turned a nigga into a minute man. Give me a little time to get myself together then I can make it up to you in the next round," Byron said as he rolled over onto his back.

Chyna sat there for a couple of minutes, looking dumbfounded until she heard snoring. She thanked God that Byron had passed out. She knew he was going to be sleep for a while, and she only promised him two hours. It's not her fault he fell asleep.

Chyna got dressed in a hurry but quietly and went back up to her bedroom. As soon as she made it to her room, she called

Josh's phone. She hadn't seen or answered any of his calls since the fight she had with Iesha. She was horny and needed to come. Since Maddox was back in Atlanta, Josh was going to have to do.

"Hello?" Josh answered on the first ring.

"Hey, are you busy?"

"No, I was about to head home."

"Do you want to come meet me at The Westin downtown?"

"Yeah, text me the room number. I should be there in about twenty minutes."

"Alright," Chyna said as she hung up the phone and sent him the room number.

Chyna walked into the bathroom and took a quick shower and brushed her teeth. She couldn't believe Byron's sex game was that weak. He couldn't even make her cum from eating her pussy. She was convinced that the bitches acted crazy over him because of his money or they pussy was trash.

Chyna brushed her hair into a ponytail just as there was a knock at the door. She put her robe on then walked to answer the door. Chyna looked through the door to make sure that it was Josh then opened it up.

"Hey, baby, I missed you," said Josh.

"Hey, I missed you too," Chyna replied truthfully.

"So, you're ready to talk about what happened now?"

"No, there's nothing to talk about. I'm just ready for you to make me cum," Chyna purred as she dropped the robe, showing her naked body.

Josh wasted no time stripping out of his clothes and crashing his lips into Chyna's. Before she could react, he had her pushed upside the door and his head buried deep inside of her honey pot in one swift move. Chyna held onto the back of Josh's head and allowed him to take care of his business. She was always told the toxic niggas was the ones that dicked you down the best, and that's exactly what Josh was. He was eating her out so good, her toes were curling. After making her come twice, he lifted her up and fucked her against the door until he was nutting deep inside of her.

After they both caught their breaths, they took it to the bedroom to pick up where they left off at in the living room. They ended up fucking for almost two hours until they fell asleep in each other's arms.

❦ 15 ❦

ONE YEAR LATER

The past year had gone by fast for Chyna. She had been heavy in the streets; she was at the point where her and her team was bringing in over sixty-five thousand dollars after the fourth month, and she was making even more money now that she'd expanded her business. In the beginning, things were kind of slow, and she needed to get the hang of things. Mase saw potential in her, so he took her under his wing. He taught her better strategies to get her product out in the street. He taught her how to be persuasive without even actually having to fuck somebody or compromise herself. Once she mastered that, she was seeing more money and going to Mase quicker for product, which was making him more money in the process. He decided to do a trial period with her, and she started pushing ketamine, sour diesel, and Moon rocks. Soon, she had become a pro and had regulars. She went from selling a gram to three point five or better. She even had some people that bought ounces from her.

Yakea and Robin were in charge of selling the pills while Tess and her brother, Tre, were taking care of the weed. Then, there were two young cats from out West that Mase put her in contact with that sold the ketamine and moon rocks. It stayed that way up until two months ago where she ended up with an even larger team.

Chyna really didn't want more than her original six people, but she was pushing more products and getting even more money. She had now ventured out to pushing dope and weight, thanks to a proposition from her father and brother. She had kept her hustling from her family for the first six months, then she went on and told Rome about it because all she thought about was getting the money. She had never fully thought about how to clean it and get it inside of an account, being that she was only eighteen years old at the time. She couldn't just go to the bank and deposit thousands of dollars a week with no job. That would have been an automatic red flag.

She had started renting out a store front, and the first thing she did was have the office remodeled. She had a wall vault put in that gave the illusion of a bookcase, to store her drugs and half of her money. The other half was in a safe that she had in her closet at home. To the naked eye, it seemed like a regular bookcase that she put her personal items and books on. She knew that was only a temporary fix because it wasn't smart to leave dope and that much money in an office, whether it was in a safe or not.

Chyna had come clean with her father three months ago on her nineteenth birthday. She'd only told him because her store was about to open soon, and the first thing that had come to his mind was where did she get the money from. She had also been in the process of finding a condo because she was serious about not staying with her parents longer than needed. She didn't even want them to try and come up with an excuse as to why she couldn't move, so she wanted it to be known that she had her own money.

When Mr. Black first found out about what Chyna was doing, he was furious and kicked her out. Instead of her getting mad or arguing, she packed a suitcase and went to stay with Josh, which only pissed her father and Rome off. They hated the fact that she was in a back and forth relationship with him. She and Josh had actually started a relationship about a month after he came to her hotel room, when she had the meeting with Mase and the girls. Everything was going good for about seven months, then she decided to break things off with him. They had ended on good terms, so they were still friends with benefits. That was what worked for both of them and prevented them from hurting each other in the process. That's why when she told him she needed a temporary place to stay, he welcomed her with no questions asked. He knew that she wasn't going to turn him down, so he'd have in-house pussy.

Things probably would have worked out for them if it wasn't for Iesha and Maddox. Iesha had started overdoing her part; she always seemed to find a way to insert herself into their business. She hated the fact that Josh didn't know how to put Iesha in her place. By him never checking her, it gave her the feeling that he was still fucking on her since she was still acting crazy.

Chyna didn't trip about the situation because around that same time, Maddox had moved to Chicago. Josh hated their friendship because he knew that she had slept with him before, and he would do it again if he had the chance. The same way she felt about Iesha was the same way Josh felt about Maddox. She would have actually stayed with Maddox when her father put her out, but he was just getting situated in his apartment, and she didn't want to bring the unnecessary attention to him. She was already in enough shit on her own.

Chyna's father, along with Rome and Maddox, had a meeting with her when he allowed her to come back home. They wanted to know how her operation worked and who was involved. He didn't agree with what she was doing, but he had to admit she was smart about it. He couldn't just knowingly have her out there getting money in the streets like that without the proper protection. That was when he came up with the proposition for her that expanded her business. Since Maddox had just moved to town and was expanding their business, he suggested that she team up with him. All the work that she was pushing would be combined with everything Maddox would be pushing out. That would also mean she was venturing into dope, which was starting to bring more money her way. He explained that she was seeing too much money to not have some hittas on her team. It would have been only a matter of time before a nigga started hating that a female was bringing in more money than them in the drug game.

Chyna was able to keep her same workers, but now they were considered to be part of her father's organization as well, but under her and Maddox along with ten other people in charge of various tasks as well. It actually worked out better for Chyna because she was able to move her product from the store and into one of the warehouses. She was scheduled to have a grand opening in a month. All of the renovations were done already, and she was just waiting on the shipment of clothes and hair. She had to hire a manager, and Bri was an assistant manager, so she wasn't comfortable with having drugs in a place with innocent people.

On top of everything that was going on with the business, Chyna was proud of herself. She didn't allow anything that was going on in her life to interfere with her schoolwork. She had finished the school year off with a three point eight GPA and was already on a good start with her second year.

Chyna had put on a pair of black leggings and a white t-shirt with a pair of black Air Max. She was in the process of brushing her hair into a ponytail when her phone started ringing. She looked down at the phone and saw that it was Maddox.

"Hello," answered Chyna.

"Hey, I'm outside your house. Are you ready?"

"I'll be out in two minutes," Chyna replied before hanging up the phone.

Chyna grabbed her backpack from the bed then headed down the stairs where she found her mother sitting down watching TV.

"I'm about to go, I'll be back later on," said Chyna.

"Where are you going?" asked Mrs. Black.

"I'm going to do some training with Maddox then we're going to the warehouse after that to check a shipment," replied Chyna.

"Be careful, I wish you would just leave this stuff to the men and focus on school. I still can't believe your father is allowing you to work with them now."

"I'll be careful. See you later, Ma, I love you."

"I love you too."

Chyna walked outside to Maddox's silver Lexus truck and climbed in, throwing her bag in the back seat.

"Do you have everything that you need for tonight or you're going to have to come back here?"

"Nah, my change of clothes and stuff in my book bag. I'll just shower at your house before we go to the warehouse."

"Alright," Maddox replied as he drove towards the gym.

The training that she did with Rome was now done with Maddox as well. She went from working out and training once a week to almost three or four times a week. She still did one day with Rome, but the other days were with Maddox. They stayed at the gym for almost two hours before leaving and grabbing food then heading to his house. When they walked into the house, Matteo was lying across the couch watching TV.

"Hey, Matt," spoke Chyna.

"Hey, Chy, do I need to go to my room and put headphones in?"

"Nah, your brother not fucking with me like that no more. It is what it is though," shrugged Chyna.

"Really, Chy, you know exactly why I'm not. If you want to finally have the conversation about us, then we can go in my bedroom and talk about it. I won't put your personal business out there for my brother to hear."

"There's nothing to talk about. Can we just eat, so that I can shower and take a nap before we go?" asked Chyna.

"Sorry, I asked," mumbled Matteo.

Maddox chuckled at his brother while Chyna ignored him and went and sat at their table. She took a couple pieces of chicken from the pan and put them on a plate along with some French fries. She played a game and texted on her phone while eating and ignored everything he was saying.

"I know you fucking hear me talking to you!" Maddox yelled as he snatched her phone out of her hand and read her text message that had just came in from Josh.

"Give me my shit back!" Chyna yelled as she jumped up in his face.

"Sit your ass down and act like you hear me. I don't give a fuck about you being mad, I'm talking to you about shit for tonight, so put your feelings in your pocket."

"Man, you want the phone, keep it. I don't have time for this shit," Chyna fumed as she rushed past him and went to the bathroom in his room.

Chyna slammed the door and stripped from her clothes then climbed into the shower. She closed her eyes and allowed the hot water to run over her face and entire body. She was finishing up when the shower door slid open, and Maddox climbed in.

"What the fuck is your problem, Chyna? Why you acting like you don't know why we not together?"

"Get the fuck out of here. I'm not trying to hear your reasoning."

"My reasoning? You acting like the shit isn't valid though. Why the fuck do we have to hide you fucking around with me, but everyone knew about you and Josh? Then you acting like I just wanted to fuck you. I told you be with me, and we could go sit down and talk to your brother and father, but you said no. You weren't ready for a relationship with me yet."

"Yeah, I said that because what the fuck I look like going to sit down with my father and telling him that me and you gone be together, knowing that you're already fucking around with two bitches in the organization and no telling how many other ones outside because I know three all together for a fact."

"Don't act like I didn't tell you. If you gave me a chance, I would have dropped those two that I was dealing with at the time."

"Yeah, but then, right after that, you went and fucked Tess, Mad. You fucked a bitch that works for me and who's face I have to see damn near every day. You got her ass walking around in love with you and shit. Then not only that, I have to see you hugged up or hear her talk about how good y'all sex is? I mean, I guess knowing you haven't given her head lightens the blow some, but damn. We're not in a relationship, but you know that I love you, Maddox. There's supposed to be a level of respect to it. I don't throw Josh in your face ever, and you'd never hear about how my sex is with him."

"Yeah, I might not hear about how y'all sex is, but you don't think I feel a certain type of way knowing that nigga can hit whenever he wants to? When I'm the only one that should be sliding up in you, but you rejected me? All of this is on you, Chyna."

"You know what, fuck you, Mad!" Chyna screamed as she muffed him and tried to climb out of the shower, so he wouldn't see her tears, but he grabbed her by her hair and slammed her into the shower wall.

Maddox stood looking at Chyna for a minute. They both had done things over the last couple of months to hurt each other. He knew that he was wrong for having sex with Tess, but that was the same day that Chyna rejected him, so he was drunk and not thinking straight, then after that it just continued to happen. The sex with her wasn't even all that good to him. She gave good head, and it was a quick nut.

"When was the last time you let that nigga hit?" Maddox asked through gritted teeth.

"None of your damn business. I don't ask you when the last time you fucked one of your bitches," said Chyna.

"A week ago, now answer my question," Maddox said through gritted teeth as he pulled her hair harder.

"It's been a month, now let me go!" yelled Chyna.

Maddox removed his hand from Chyna's hair then took a step back.

"Oh, so that's your problem. You need to cum, so you're taking your anger out on me. What's wrong? It's his other girl-friend turn, right now?"

"Wow, get the fuck out of my face!" Chyna yelled as she slapped the shit out of him and climbed out of the shower. She wrapped a towel around her body and walked inside of the bedroom with Maddox right behind her.

Chyna sat on the bed, so she could put her lotion on and ignored everything that Maddox was saying. He had just hit below the belt and all bets were off. Maddox dropped to his knees in front of her.

"I am so sorry, I shouldn't have said that. I took it too far; me and you are better than that. We were friends before anything, and I never meant to hurt you. I'll call things off with Tess tonight," said Maddox.

Chyna continued to ignore him until he picked up one of her legs and threw it over his shoulder.

"Stop it, Mad, you remember you not fucking with me like that," was the last words Chyna got out before his mouth was on her clit. She instantly grabbed the back of his head and allowed him to devour her pussy. She was still mad at him, but she was sexually frustrated and in need of some dick.

Maddox continued to give her head until her legs started shaking, and she was cumming in his mouth. He reached over and grabbed a Magnum from the nightstand and put it on before sliding deep inside of her, causing a moan to escape both of their lips. He lifted her from the bed and sat on the chair in his room, so she could ride him. She closed her eyes and rode him nice and slow. He latched on her neck with his teeth and bit down gently, causing her to cry out in ecstasy.

"Damn, I missed you, this shit feel so good. Please forgive me, you know I love you," Maddox groaned as she rotated her hips slowly.

Her shit was wet as hell and had him ready to bust already, but he knew that he needed to hold out. He wanted to savor the moment because there was no telling when she'd fuck him again. She hadn't touched him since she'd found out he was sleeping with Tess.

Chyna rode Maddox until she was cumming, then turned around in a reversed style and picked up the pace. She knew just how he like it and what it took to make him cum. He had made her come three times already, and she was tired from the long day she had and needed a nap because they were about to have a longer night. About five minutes later, he was cumming into the condom.

Chyna climbed off of him and went into the bathroom to wash her kitty with soap and water then went back inside of his bedroom.

"I'm still mad at you," Chyna said.

"I know, but I promise to make things right between us."

"Don't make promises you can't keep. Now, when's the last time you changed your sheets?"

"I just changed them last night when I did laundry, but I haven't had sex with anybody in my bed if that's why you're asking. You're the only female that I allow in my house. Hell, don't none of them even know where I live at. I'm not trying to have no bitch set me up," said Maddox.

"Okay, well set your alarm, so that we can get up in two hours. Your ass wants to be energizer bunny and shit. You done messed up our nap time."

"Shut up, you know you loved every bit of it," Maddox said as he pulled Chyna close to him and kissed the back of her head.

❧ 16 ❧

Chloe laid across her bed, huffing and puffing while trying to catch her breath.

Nathan had just finished giving her some of the best sex they'd had since they'd first gotten married. They had been having sex damn near every night. She didn't know what was going on with him, but he had been bringing his A-game. He had taken her on a romantic dinner, and the night ended with them making love.

"I'm about to go get us some water, then we can take a shower and watch a movie," said Nathan.

Nathan walked into the kitchen and grabbed a bottle of water, then walked back to his bedroom.

"Babe, somebody named Jaden keeps calling. Do you want me to answer it?" Chloe asked, holding up the phone.

"No, it's fine, it's just someone from work. I'll call him back in a minute. Why don't you go start the shower while I change the sheets, then I'll be there to join you?"

"Alright, don't make me wait long," flirted Chloe.

Once Nathan heard the shower door close and the water running, he stepped into the hallway and called "Jaden from work" back.

"Now, you know how to call me back!" Jade snapped into the phone.

"I've been busy with my wife all day. Why the fuck is you calling me while I'm at home anyway? I thought I made it clear the beginning of this month that what we had was over?"

"Nah, it doesn't work that way. You don't get to use me and then just throw me away with no warning. We have some shit to discuss, so you need to meet me at my house tomorrow around noon. If you don't meet me there, then I might have to have the conversation with your wife instead," Jade threatened before hanging up the phone on him.

Nathan kicked himself for still fucking with Jade. In the beginning, he had only did it that one time like he said he would, but he couldn't get her off his mind. Then, a couple months went by, and he did it again until it turned into a weekly thing, and he was paying one of her monthly bills.

Everything was going good with them for a few months until she started talking about how she was falling in love with him and that he should leave his wife to be with her. It was like she was forgetting what her place was. He was convinced that she was crazy; like *A Thin Line Between Love and Hate* crazy. He had even tried calling things off with her, but she threatened to tell Chloe that they were messing around if he didn't continue to pay her bill and have sex with her weekly.

Nathan didn't want any problems with Chloe, so he agreed to Jade's demands. It seemed like things were getting better up until the beginning of the month when she started calling his phone all times of the day and getting mad if he didn't answer. He was convinced that she was on some drugs or something because he didn't know what made her snap that way. Since she didn't keep up her end of the deal and stay in her place, he didn't keep hers. Now, that she was back calling him, he needed to go and pay her a visit the next day to see what she needed to talk about.

Nathan hung up the phone and silenced it then walked back

into the bedroom and changed the sheets before joining Chloe in the shower.

"Is everything alright, baby?" Chloe asked.

"Yeah, he was letting me know that he has an emergency, and he won't be in to work tonight."

"Awe okay, so you're going to have to go in?" she inquired, sounding a little disappointed.

"No, I contacted one of the other workers and asked if they wanted to do overtime, therefore, I'm all yours," Nathan said as he kissed her gently on the lips.

Nathan and Chloe finished washing each other up then headed to the bedroom where they laid down and found a movie to watch. Once the movie was over, it was pretty late, so they called it a night.

The following morning, Chloe and Nathan got up and headed to work. Nathan made sure to go in early since he was going to take a longer lunch. He just hoped that Jade didn't hit him with no bullshit. The day was going by fast and around eleven, he received a call from Chloe.

"Hey, baby," Nathan answered.

"Hey love, I was trying to see if you wanted to meet up for lunch today?"

"I wish I could, but I'm swamped with work and meetings. I'll most likely be working through lunch," Nathan lied.

He hated that he had to lie to his wife because he was finally back to doing right by her. He couldn't wait until his talk with Jade was over with. No matter what she told him, he was done dealing with her for good. He was going to block her number for good. He was glad that she didn't know where he lived or worked.

Once it was noon, Nathan let his secretary know that he was done for the day, and he headed to Jade's house. Nathan parked his car then walked up the few steps to her apartment and knocked on the door.

"Hey, Nate, glad you didn't take my threat lightly," said Jade.

"I don't have time for this shit. I have to get back to work. What's so important for us to talk about?"

"Wow, is that the way to talk to the person that gave you the best sex of your life? You know you hurt me, Nate. I really do love you, but you just threw me away like I wasn't shit."

"Please stop it with the theatrics, Jade. You knew I was married from the beginning, and you had no problem with that. I know that you were sleeping with other people as well, but now all of a sudden, I'm supposed to believe that you love me?"

"You can believe whatever you want. At the end of the day, I'm pregnant, and it's yours," Jade said, throwing a piece of paper in his face.

"Bullshit, you might be pregnant, but it's not mine. I strapped up every time!" yelled Nate.

"Well, the last couple of times we had sex, I may or may not have put the condom on you. I needed to find a way to break you and your wife up, so that you could be with me, and this was the only way."

"You stupid bitch, get rid of the fucking baby! I'm not leaving my wife for your ass."

"Yeah, we'll see about that," Jade sneered.

Nathan gave her a look of disgust then walked out of the house and to his car. He hit his fist against the steering wheel because he couldn't realize how he had been so stupid. He had no idea what he was going to do now. All he could picture was him losing his wife over some bullshit. Nathan called his secretary to let her know he wasn't coming back in for the day and headed to his father's house. He needed to talk to his father and see what he should do. Nathan pulled up to his father's house and climbed out of the car. He rang the doorbell and waited a few minutes for him to come to the door.

"Hey, son," Mr. Tanner spoke.

"Hey pops, how are you doing?" Nathan asked as he embraced him into a hug.

"I'm happy to see you, but what are you doing here in the

middle of the day unannounced? I was actually about to head out in a few minutes to meet up with Big Rome at the warehouse."

"It won't take long, pops. I just need your opinion on what to do. I fucked-up big time," said Nathan.

"Okay, tell me what you did."

"I've been sleeping around with somebody else off and on for the past year. I've tried to end it multiple times, but then she started talking about that she loves me and that if I stopped seeing her, she would tell Chloe, so I just continued. She kept blowing up my phone last night after me not talking to her for a month, saying she needed to speak with me. I went to her house today, and her ass showed me a paper showing that she was pregnant, and it's mine. She said that whenever we had sex the last couple of times, she didn't put on a condom or she was either slipping it off."

"Man, how could you be so stupid? It was stupid of you to sleep around on your wife. It was even more stupid to stick your dick back in her after she told you that she loved you. It doesn't matter that she said she would tell your wife. Bitches like that would leave you alone if you threw some money her way. You should have paid her ass off and cut ties with her."

"Okay, but that does me no good now that she's pregnant. I told her to get an abortion, but I know she's not."

"You damn right, she won't because that baby will be her meal ticket. You need to cut all ties with her completely. Make up an excuse to Chloe about why you need a new number and be the best husband that you can be. You're going to act like the conversation with ole girl never even happened."

"What about the baby though? What if it's mine?"

"Which do you want more, a baby with your outside bitch or your marriage to fail?"

"You know I don't want my marriage to fail. I love my wife, not to mention, what Rome and Mr. Black would do to me."

"Okay then, keep your mouth shut and act like nothing

happened. If and when it ever comes up down the line, play dumb the entire time," Mr. Tanner advised.

"Alright pops, thanks for the advice. I'll text you my new number when I get it."

"Okay son, be safe," Mr. Tanner replied.

Nathan sent Chloe a text message, letting her know that his last meeting of the day was canceled, so he'd be home early. He went to the floral shop and bought her a dozen roses then went home and started dinner. He wanted everything to be ready by time she got home. Operation best husband in the world was activated and in full effect.

❧ 17 ☙

"**O**h my, God, Maddox," Chyna moaned as he sucked on her love box. He was making her come in his mouth for the second time.

"You have to be quiet before someone hears us," Maddox whispered as he pulled his dick out and slid up inside of her. A moan instantly escaped both of their mouths. He smashed his lips into hers to try and muffle the sounds that she was making. Chyna was never quiet when they had sex, so he didn't know why he expected anything different that day.

Chyna and Maddox had just finished weighing and bagging up some of the product that needed to be distributed. Once they finished, they went to her office to go over some paperwork since they had to wait for some of the workers to finish with a shipment anyway. They went from chilling to him asking if he could just taste it, to him beating her pussy up.

"Right there, baby, please don't stop, you about to make me cummmm!" Chyna cried.

"Fuck, I'm right behind you," Maddox growled.

"Don't cum in me," Chyna commanded as she pushed him back.

"Damn it, Chy, I wasn't about to come in you, now you just

fucked my nut up," Maddox hissed as he started stroking his dick.

"I'm sorry," Chyna replied as she climbed from the desk and put his dick in her mouth. It only took about five minutes until he was ready to cum again.

"Shit, I'm about to cum!" Maddox exclaimed as he dropped his load down Chyna's throat. He looked down at her as she swallowed every drop.

Chyna stood from the floor and wiped the side of her mouth then leaned over in her desk drawer to get a feminine wipe to clean herself and handed one to Maddox as well. She was in the process of wiping herself when there was a knock at her door.

"Who is it?" Chyna called out.

"It's me!" Rome yelled.

"Give me one minute," Chyna replied as she hurriedly fixed her clothes and sprayed a little freshener in the air. Once Maddox saw that she had stopped panicking, he opened the door for Rome.

"What's up, Rome? What are you doing here?" Chyna asked as she lit a blunt.

"I had been calling your phone to let you know I was stopping by, but you didn't answer."

"Sorry about that, I forgot to take my phone off silent when I finished dealing with the product."

Chyna always silenced her phone when she was weighing or counting the money, so she wouldn't get distracted, so she figured that was a believable story.

"Okay, cut the bullshit. Are y'all two sleeping together?" Rome questioned.

"Why would you ask that?" Chyna questioned, pretending to be shocked.

"That's not an answer to my question, Chyna," Rome replied calmly.

"Yes, we are," said Maddox.

"What the hell! Why would you say something!" Chyna snapped.

"Come on now, Chyna. If he asked, that means he already has an idea. I told you that I would not voluntarily tell since you didn't want me to, but you can't expect me to just lie in his face. How do you think that would make me look in the end?"

"Don't get mad at him. Why didn't you tell me? We used to be able to talk about damn near everything. You don't trust me anymore or something?" Rome inquired.

"Of course, I trust you, Rome. You're the one person I trust the most in this world. Some things I have to be able to figure out on my own without always running to my big brother. That's why it took me a minute to come to you and let you know what I was doing in the streets. As far as the situation with Maddox goes, I'm nineteen now. You can't expect me to talk to you about my sex life. I already know how you feel about Josh. I didn't need you judging me about two men."

"I'm sorry that you feel that way. I would never judge you, but I understand where you coming from and now that I think about it, I could see why you didn't want to tell me. I do have to give my input that this shit can turn bad with him sleeping with you and Tess."

"I broke things off with Tess a week ago. I should have never started sleeping with her. I had asked your sister to be with me, but she didn't want you to know, so she rejected me. I was pissed and finally gave into Tess' advances. Plus, I hated that she was still dealing with Josh."

"Well, y'all need to get y'all shit together because there's other people involved."

"Yeah, you're right," Chyna replied.

They stood and talked for a little while until Chyna and Maddox left so they could head home. Maddox walked with Chyna to her car and leaned up against her.

"Come home with me, tonight," Maddox whispered in her ear.

"No, I'm tired as shit. I need to take a shower and get some sleep."

"We can shower together and then go to sleep. We don't have to do anything else if you don't feel like it," Maddox said.

Chyna contemplated what Maddox was saying. She could go for just some relaxation in the comfort of his arms.

"Cuddling only," Chyna warned.

"Great," Maddox said he started to suck on her neck.

"See, you can't be doing that when I get to your house, or it won't be no sleeping," laughed Chyna.

"Okay, I promise, I won't try anything. Well, at least until after we get some sleep," Maddox smirked.

"So, that's why you abruptly called shit off with me? You fucking with her now!" Tess yelled.

"Chill, Tess, me and you were never in a relationship. I can count on one hand how many times we've had sex. I've never even took you out on a date," said Maddox.

"How could you do this to me, Chyna? You're supposed to be my friend, and you started fucking him behind my back."

"It's not even like that. You can calm down, and we can talk about this tomorrow," Chyna suggested.

"No, we gone talk about this shit right now because I thought we were better than that. This was some hoe shit you just pulled!" Tess snapped.

Chyna stood there calmly and maintained composure because had it been anybody else, Tess would've gotten socked in the mouth already.

"I'm going to need you to pipe the fuck down and realize who you're talking to. Let's not get shit twisted. You're cool and all, but don't forget that you work for me. I don't owe your ass an explanation, but I'll be nice and let you know that I didn't fuck Maddox behind your back. I've been dealing with Mad for over a year, it just wasn't anybody else's business."

"My fault, you right," Tess said as she nodded her head and walked away.

"So, are you still coming to my house?" Maddox asked, causing Chyna to laugh.

"Yeah fool, I'll follow you," Chyna chuckled.

Maddox and Chyna went to his house, and he kept his promise. They took a shower and went to bed. He definitely made up not trying anything the night before though because that following afternoon, he had woken her up with his head buried between her thighs and dicked her down for hours. Once they were done, she made them lunch then headed home so she could get some studying done before doing pickups that evening.

Chyna was lying across her bed, studying when her father ducked his head into her room.

"You got a minute to talk?" he asked.

"Yeah, I was just finishing up anyway. I have to get dressed in a few minutes."

"You know that I love you, Chyna, and I love your drive. I've haven't seen anybody push themselves as much as you do since I started this organization. I know you hated how strict I was and thought that I was being mean. I never meant to push you to the point that you would do this. The truth is I saw a lot of me inside of you and that scared the shit out of me that my baby girl was a beast like that. I didn't want this life for you; your brother kept telling me that the route I went with Chloe wouldn't work for you. You've always been beautiful and smart, so I didn't want to think that he was right. I guess, I just wanted to say that I'm sorry if I failed you as a father. There's not a day that goes by that I don't worry about you while you're out in these streets. These niggas are jealous and hateful, baby girl. I'm not telling you to stop what you're doing. I just want you to be careful and move smart. Think about what's your end goal and what's it going to take for you to slow down some because I know for a fact that you have enough money stacked to live comfortably for a few years. You don't want to get too caught up in the fast life that you forget to live and enjoy the fruit of your labor."

"Dad, you did not fail me as a parent. Yes, I used to hate how strict you were, but I realize you were only trying your best to protect me, and I respect you for that. The thing is, when I figured it out, it was already too late. It didn't matter how strict you were though, I've never seen a nine to five in my future. I knew from the beginning that I wanted to be a part of your organization. Hell, it was my birthright. I can say that I probably jumped into it a little faster than I would have if I didn't feel like every aspect of my life was being controlled. Rome was right, and he knew from the beginning. Chloe and I are opposite people and the more you tried to do the things that you did to her, made me even more rebellious. I knew that I was destined for greatness. You and mom taught be that at a very young age. I needed to be able to say that I got the bread that I was seeing off of my own name and not because I was the daughter of Big Rome. I plan on slowing down for a few months, so that I can get my store up and running smoothly. I might not let it show, but I appreciate everything you've done for me, and I actually listen to you. I love you, daddy, and that will never change," Chyna said as a tear fell from her eyes.

Mr. Black leaned in and hugged his daughter and kissed her on the forehead.

"I won't hold you up any longer. I know that you need to be meeting up with Maddox soon. If you're not coming home tonight, please call," stated Mr. Black.

"Okay I will, but I'll most likely be home tonight," Chyna said as she climbed out the bed.

Chyna looked in her drawer and pulled out a pair of black jeans with a black V-neck shirt and her black Prada sneakers. She went into the bathroom and took a quick shower then got dressed. Since they were going to do pickups, she brushed her hair into a ponytail and put on her hat. She grabbed her purse from the bag then headed out of the house to her car.

❧ 18 ❧

Chyna pulled up to Maddox's house, and he came right down the stairs. It took them two hours to drive to all of their spots to collect the money. They had finally pulled up to the last spot of the night. They drove around to the back, and MJ came running to the car with a bag of money.

"What the hell is up with your girl, Tess? I called her a couple hours ago and told her that we were down to our last couple of bags, and she said she was on her way but never showed up. Now, we dry, and I have someone that's supposed to come get a half-ounce in about an hour, not to mention, everybody else that's looking for weed. Should I tell him don't come?"

"Nah, you can tell him to come. We'll go grab you some and be back in thirty minutes," said Maddox.

"Bet, good looking out, Mad, just hit the horn when you get back."

Chyna remained silent the entire ride to Maddox's house.

"What are we doing at your house?"

"I got a couple pounds of weed here, so I thought I could grab it instead of going all the way back to the warehouse, that way, we'll be back in time."

"Are you out of your mind? Since when do we deliver drugs to spots? We have people on payroll for that shit."

"Yeah, but he said she haven't answering, so we just supposed to keep losing out on money?"

"I'm not trying to hear that shit, Maddox. Go in the house and get the half- ounce only. We'll call and see can we get in touch with Tess or Tre to go pick up the rest from the drop off spot to take them. I'm not about to ride around with all this shit. As a matter of fact, take all the money we collected in with you. We can count that shit we get back. Something don't seem right about this."

"Alright, I'll be right back," said Maddox.

"Okay, don't take all day. I'm hungry, we're supposed to be going to get food now," pouted Chyna.

Maddox shook his head and climbed out of the car. Chyna sat and played on her phone until Maddox came back down.

"Aye, get in the driver's seat, so that I can call roll up. I talked to Tess, and she said that she was still taking care of something with Tre, so I told her don't worry about it. We'd take care of it."

Chyna rolled her eyes and climbed over into the driver seat then headed back towards the spot.

"Man, fuck that, she wasn't slacking before she found out about us two. If she doesn't want to work anymore, then she need to just say something. We can't be missing out on money because of her."

"I know, let's just take care of this, and if she's not done by time we finish eating, we can have somebody else take care of it."

Chyna was about two blocks away at a stoplight when she noticed a detective's truck behind her. She made sure to adhere to all of the traffic stops, so she wouldn't get pulled over. The light turned green, and she picked up the speed. She looked back in the mirror and noticed that he had slowed down, so she shrugged it off and made a turn onto the block. She had made another turn into the alley when she noticed a police car behind her.

"Aye, don't turn around, but there's a cop behind us. Don't make any sudden moods, but I have a feeling that they're about to pull us over. I'm going to bypass the house, so that they don't have a reason to run up in there."

"Just relax, Chy, you can just be paranoid."

"I'm not; I have a gut feeling about this shit. I told you it was a bad idea when you suggested we go get the shit."

Chyna drove pass the trap house and turned the corner to go back to the main street when the police turned their lights on.

"Shit, I got my piece on me."

"Act like you're getting my registration out of the glove compartment and stick the gun in there. Then hand me the weed with my purse," said Chyna.

"What?"

"Just do it, please. I'll take the wrap," Chyna pleaded as she cracked her window.

"Get the fuck out of the car!" the officer yelled as he pulled on her door handle.

Chyna and Maddox opened the door and climbed out. The police threw them against the car and handcuffed them both. They were only standing there for about a minute when another police car pulled up, flashing their lights along with two detectives. The officers cuffed them then put them in separate police cars. Chyna sat in the back of the police car, pissed that she hadn't followed her first mind. Her gut had told her not to come back, and she should have listened.

After sitting in the car for about five minutes, a woman detective walked up to the car.

"We found some weed and a gun. Who does it belong to?"

"It's mine," Chyna confessed.

"Bullshit, I'll ask one more time, then I'm going to haul your ass down to the station with your little boyfriend. Who does the gun belong to?"

"I just told you that it's mine."

"Okay, have it your way," the detective stated before walking away.

Chyna watched as the polices went all through her car and trunk like they were on a mission to find more than what they had found. The police came to the car and yanked Chyna out and pushed her back up against the car.

"I know you have more than that little shit we found in your purse. Where is the rest of it?" the officer fumed.

"I don't know what you're talking about," Chyna replied calmly.

"I guess, I need to search you then." The officer smirked as his hands roamed all over Chyna's body. He even stuck his hand down inside of her pants and underwear.

"Get the fuck of me. You're not allowed to search me!" Chyna yelled.

"Shut the fuck up!" he yelled as he slapped the shit out of her, causing blood to drip from her lip.

"Are you out of your mind? Get your hands off her and put her back in the car," his partner hissed as he stormed over to them.

The side of Chyna's face stung, but she refused to show any weakness. She bit the inside of her jaw to calm down. After about another ten minutes of searching her car, one of the detectives climbed in and drove it away. She noticed that they didn't let Maddox out of the other police car, so that meant they were taking him down to the station too. She just hoped that he kept his mouth shut. He had already had a possession charge before, so he would have gotten more time than her. She had a clean record, and it would be her first offense, so she prayed a lawyer could get her off with probation or just a year.

Chyna entered the station, and they fingerprinted her and closed her away in an interrogation room, where they kept her in there for damn near three hours before coming to question her.

"Sorry about the hold up, we're kind of busy. Can I get anything for you?"

"Yeah, my lawyer," said Chyna.

"Okay, but first, I just have a few questions for you. What do you know about The Black Renaissance, and where is their warehouse?"

"I'm sorry; I'm not sure what that is. Is that some kind of new hotel or something?" Chyna inquired with a straight face.

"I know you, know what that is. From what we know, it's ran by a Roman Sr., and Roman Jr. is next in line. I know that's your father and brother, so just tell me what you know, and I'll have all charges dropped against you."

"My father is a respective businessman. He has a few businesses that he runs out here along with my brother. As far as a Black Renaissance goes, I've never heard of that a day in my life."

Chyna could tell that the detective was pissed because he slammed his hands onto the table and stood up, leaning in her face.

"Cut the fucking act already. I know that you know what it is, and I also know that you're a part of it now. So, just tell me where y'all keep the drugs and weapons that y'all distribute. Make this easier on you than it has to be. You're too beautiful for jail. You know how many women would jump to the occasion to make you their bitch?"

"I am a fulltime student at the University of Chicago with a three point eight GPA. I don't even have time to be in the streets like that, let alone be a part of an organization. I don't partake in any kind of distribution of guns or weapons."

"Okay, so how do you explain the drugs and gun we found in your car?"

"That's simple; I had just come back from the range and was on my way home to put my gun away. As far as the weed goes, that was only a half of an ounce. That was my personal stash which I had just bought and was about to take that in the house as well. Now, can you please call my lawyer?"

The officer looked like he wanted to smack the shit out of

Chyna, but he knew that he wouldn't be able to get away with it, so he stormed out of the room, leaving her alone for another two hours. A female officer entered the room, asking Chyna the same exact questions as the previous officer, but in a different way, and she pissed her off just as much as she did the previous officer.

"I get it, you're trying to be the perfect daughter and girlfriend, so you're keeping your mouth closed. You know what's going to happen when you're behind bars? Everyone is going to go on with their lives like you never existed. That boyfriend of yours will have a new girl in his bed before you're able to plea anything. He's not going to wait on you, and jail isn't a place for a beautiful girl like you. I know that you're smarter than this," the officer continued to antagonize Chyna, but she never changed her facial expression. She and her family had worked too hard for her to break that easily.

"Okay, I'll tell you something," Chyna said, sitting up in her seat.

The officer picked up her ink pen, ready to write down Chyna's confession.

"Alright, I'm ready."

"I want my lawyer, right now. I've been here for over five hours and have not been able to make one phone call, and you're steady questioning me like I didn't request to speak with my lawyer."

"You stupid little girl!" the officer yelled as the door swung open. A man in a suit along with the lieutenant entered the room.

"Give them the room, this is her attorney," the lieutenant ordered.

"Are you alright?" Mr. Arnold asked as he examined Chyna's face, noticing it was swollen as well as her lips.

Mr. Arnold was her family lawyer; her father paid a hefty retainer for his services.

"No, I'm not okay, I'm being held here for more than what the fuck they found in my car. They keep asking me about dope, guns, warehouses, and some organization called Black Renaissance. I told them repeatedly that I don't know what that is. Then on top of that, I've been requesting to call you for the past five hours, and they haven't even let me make a phone call. Also, to make matters worse, I was violated by one of the perverted officers that arrested me. He not only searched me, but he stuck his hand down my pants and into my underwear then slapped the shit out of me. Hence, the busted lip and red face. How did you know I was here?"

"Maddox called me a couple hours ago. I had been taking care of things with him, and he got released since they didn't have anything on you. Since you said that everything is yours, you'll have to stand before a judge to get bailed out."

"Let me guess, since it's a Saturday, I'm stuck in here until Monday morning."

"Yes, I'll be in court at your bail hearing, and your bail will be posted before you can be put into general population at the county. Just be patient, and we'll take of the rest. I'll make sure that they allow your phone call as well as file a complaint on your behalf against the officer."

"You can file the complaint, but I don't want a phone call. I was only going to call you anyway."

"Are you sure? Your family wants to hear from you. I told them I was on my here."

"Yeah, I'm sure, just let them know that I love them, and I'll see them Monday."

"Alright, see you, Monday," Mr. Arnold said before standing up to leave the room.

Chyna sat in the interrogation room for about twenty minutes, when an officer came and led her to a cell. She entered the cell where there was only a wired frame bed with a thin ass mattress and a toilet.

"This is going to be a long two nights," Chyna said out loud as she sat on the bed and pulled her knees to her chest.

19

"For the love of God, Maddox, do we have to talk about this shit right now? It's been two damn weeks, and everyone keeps asking me how I am doing. How the fuck do y'all think I'm doing? Somebody within our team set my ass up. I told you something didn't seem right when we made it to your house to get the shit, and you said I was being paranoid. Thank God I told you to only get the three point five and to take the money in the house, or we would have been really fucked. Those officers knew that we were going to be there. That motherfucker asked where the rest of the drugs and the money was because I should have had more than what was in my purse."

"I wasn't speeding or shit, so there was no reason for me to get pulled over. He groped my body and stuck his hand inside of my pants. When I got to the station, I was locked away in a cold ass room for hours without a once single phone call or shit. Then, when they came in the room, all they kept asking me about my father and Rome doings with the Black Renaissance. I went without eating for two days because the shit they brought me wasn't worth serving a fucking rat. So, please do not ask me how I'm doing again!" Chyna yelled as tears slowly fell from her eyes.

It was the first time since everything happened that she showed an ounce of emotion to anyone. Behind closed doors, she had been crying herself to sleep since she'd made it back home. Maddox sat on Chyna's bed and pulled her onto his lap and cradled her as she cried into his chest.

"I'm so sorry that you went through that. You shouldn't have taken the wrap for me. I could have done whatever time they were going to give me. Now, you're about to have to go to trial and fight a case. You could possibly lose your scholarship behind this. You didn't have to ruin your life for me, Chyna. Why would you even do something like this?"

"I did it because I love you, Maddox. I couldn't allow you to go down when there was something that I could do to prevent it. If you would have got locked up, they would have found a way to connect other shit that had to do with my family's organization. I threw myself into the wolves' den for all of you. I have a squeaky-clean background, and I'm an A student in college. He's going to fight for me to get probation and pay a fine because I already told them I'm not talking a plea deal and plead guilty for shit. Then, it helps that a file a lawsuit against them for sexual harassment."

"I don't know how I will ever make this up to you, but I promise, I will. I love you, Chyna, and no matter what happens, I want us to be together," Maddox said as he leaned in and kissed her.

"Let's see what happens and take it from there, first. I don't want you to start a relationship with me just because I took the fall for you, and if I do get time, I don't want to be in a relationship while in there. I'd need to focus on myself and figure out what to do with getting through that time. I can't do that and worry about who you're sleeping with while I'm away. I couldn't ask you to put your life on hold for me," Chyna replied.

"But Chy—" Maddox started then stopped when she placed her finger to his lips.

"Let's just let it go and let me get through this trial, first. If

I'm found not guilty, I'll give us a try. If not, you can do whatever your heart desires while I'm away, and if it's meant to happen between us, we can work on it when I get home."

"If we were at my house, I'd be making love to you right now," Maddox whispered in her ear."

"I know, but I really wasn't up for going out. Just lay here with me for a little while," Chyna said as she laid across her bed with Maddox holding her.

Chyna hadn't realized how tired she was until she had woken up a couple hours later, still wrapped in Maddox's arms. It was the first time that she had fallen asleep since everything happened without crying herself to sleep. There was a light knock on her door.

"Come in!" Chyna called out as she sat up in bed.

"Dinner is done, are you and Maddox going to join me and your father?"

"Yeah, we'll be right down," replied Chyna.

Chyna shook Maddox lightly to wake him up.

"Damn, I didn't even realize I fell asleep."

"It's fine, my mom invited you to stay for dinner, so let's go," Chyna said as she climbed out of bed.

Chyna looked at herself in the mirror and frowned.

"Don't do that, you look beautiful," Maddox advised her, knowing what the look on her face was for.

Chyna and Maddox walked down to the dining room where Chyna's parents were sitting at the table waiting for them.

Mrs. black had made fried chicken, baked macaroni, greens, and cornbread. Everything looked amazing, but she didn't have much of an appetite.

"What do you two have planned for tonight?" asked Mrs. Black.

"I told Audrey, I'd go see the kids since they've been looking for me. I'm going to go meet up with Rome at her people's house. After that, I'll probably go stay at Maddox's house tonight. We still have some stuff to go over."

"Alright, well, if you need anything or want to talk, we're here for you," said Mrs. Black.

"I know you are, Ma," Chyna replied as she sat back in her seat.

They all continued their conversation over dinner. Maddox stayed downstairs with Chyna's father while she went up to get dressed.

"How is my daughter, Maddox? She won't talk to any of us about what's going on with her or the case. Did she say anything to you about it?"

"No, she hasn't said anything to me about the case. I believe she thinks it's her way of protecting us all."

"Why does she have to protect us? She's the youngest one out of all of us. We should be protecting her."

"I think that's the main reason why she's the one doing the protecting. They have no solid evidence and no way to tie her to anything but what they found in the car. Chyna was smart even when she was working on her own. She has never sold any piece of drug to anyone. Even when she was getting the drugs from her connect; she never picked up anything from anyone. She had people picking up and dropping off everything for her. It would be they word against hers for anything. She says that she was set up and when I sit back and think about that day and how the events played out, it was a set up. I have an idea of who it was, but I'm trying to find out if they're working on their own. As far as what happened at the police station, they tried to get information on you, Rome, and the organization. They were never able to get anything on you, and they thought that Chyna would crack under pressure, but all she did was piss them off. She just needs time to figure out what she wants to do. Just don't ask her how she's doing anymore. I just got cursed out for it," chuckled Maddox.

"Alright, I won't ask her, but I do have a personal question for you."

"What is it?" asked Maddox.

"What are your intentions with my daughter? Do you love her or are you just having fun and playing games with her like Josh is? I see the way you look at her, and I know that you two have something going on, and I know for a fact that she loves you or she never would have taken the blame. She way too loyal to the people she loves, if you ask me," added Mr. Black.

"I'm not just having fun with Chyna. I love her, and she knows it. I've asked her multiple times to be with me, but the timing is never right. I see a future with Chyna. I've seen it since the day I met her in Atlanta. I would never intentionally hurt her or play with her heart."

"I respect your honesty, and you're a good man. You're good for her. I would have preferred her with Matteo because he's her age and not involved in this lifestyle. I now know my daughter would be no good for your brother. He would not be able to keep up with her," laughed Mr. Black.

"You know it's funny you say that. You and Chyna are a lot alike and think alike. That day in Atlanta, she told me she didn't know what you were thinking and that she would turn Matteo out so fast, my father would regret ever sending him to Chicago."

Mr. Black and Maddox continued to talk for about another twenty minutes until Chyna came down the stairs in a pair of blue jeans and a white hoody with sneakers and an overnight bag. Chyna told her parents goodbye than walked out to the car with Maddox and headed to where Audrey and Rome were.

"My car should be finished at the shop tomorrow. I still can't believe they tore up the seats. You won't have to chauffer me around anymore. I still I know it's a lot for you to come all the way out here to get me from home to take me to school and then bring me back. The condo should be ready next month, but now, I'm like do I even want to sign off on it right now? What if I have to go to jail? I'm not trying to fuck up my credit by breaking a lease."

"Sign the lease and get the condo. You have a damn good

lawyer. You have to be optimistic, now."

"Yeah, you're right," Chyna replied as she leaned back in the seat.

Maddox pulled in front of Audrey's family's house, and they climbed out to meet Rome on the porch.

"Hey, baby girl, I'm glad you decided to come out. The kids have been asking if you were coming all day," said Rome.

"Yeah, I was in a better mood today, so I figured I might as well get out of the house. Plus, Maddox would have bugged me to death if I stayed in the house," smirked Chyna.

Maddox stood there and shrugged his shoulder as they entered the house. They stayed inside and spent time with them for almost two hours, then it was the kids' bedtime.

"Come on, so I can walk with you to the car. I need to talk to you for a minute anyway," said Rome.

Chyna, Rome, and Maddox headed towards his car. He climbed in, so that Chyna and Rome could talk in private.

"What's up, big bro? Tell me what's on your mind. I can see the stress line in your forehead."

"I'm just worried about you, Chy. You've completely shut everyone out. For the first time in my entire life, I don't know how to help you. I wasn't able to protect you from this."

"It's not your fault, Rome, and you don't have to worry about me. I'm a big girl, you don't have to worry about me saying anything. I would never tell on y'all. I'll get through this like I've done everything else."

"Listen to me, Chyna, it never even crossed my mind that you'd tell on me. Even if you did, I wouldn't give a fuck because if I could, I would have taken the fall, so that you never even had to step foot in the precinct. If there's anything that you need, let me know. I already paid for the repairs on the car and told them you'd be the one to pick it up."

"You didn't have to do that, Rome. I have money, I could afford to get it fixed."

"I know, but I wanted to do it for you and if there's anything else you need, just let me know."

"I will, big brother, I'm good now though. Maddox already said he won't let me fall apart, and he has enough faith for both of us that I'll get through this with no time."

"See, I knew I liked him for a reason and let him know. I don't blame him for you taking the wrap. I know why you did it."

"Thank you, at least you know why I did it because he still can't believe it. The crazy part about it is, I would do it all over again if I had to."

"I know, baby girl, and that's why you're so loved," Rome said as he pulled his sister into a hug.

"Aye, Chyna, can we talk for a minute!" Josh yelled as he walked across the street.

"Don't leave, Rome, stay right here. I don't need no shit jumping off between him and Maddox," whispered Chyna.

"What's going on? I've been trying to call you for the past two weeks. I heard what happened, and I wanted to check on you."

"Thank you, I'm good, I just haven't been in the mood to talk to people. I've been going to school and home. This is my first time out since then."

"Awe okay, so why have you suddenly just stopped talking to me? It's been almost two months since the last time I saw you," said Josh.

"I know, and it's nothing personal. I have a lot going on in my life and just needed time to think and get myself together," replied Chyna.

"Yeah, that's funny seeing as you're with him. You're back messing with him again? Are y'all in a relationship?" Josh asked, referring to Maddox.

"Josh, I'm really not in the mood for this right now. I'll call you tomorrow, and we can talk once you're calm," responded Chyna.

Josh looked like he wanted to say something but then he looked over at Rome and had second thoughts.

"Alright, Chyna, have a good night, but please call me tomorrow. You remember at one point, we were friends before anything," Josh reminded her as he started to walk away.

"Okay, baby girl, to get out of here before his crazy ass decides to come back over here. I love you, and I'll call you tomorrow so we can hang out."

"Alright, I love you more," Chyna said as she turned to open her car door.

"Chyna, look out!" Maddox screamed as gunfire erupted.

Chyna tried to duck, but it was too late. She felt hot lead enter her body, then she was being thrown to the ground with Rome laying on top of her.

"No, no, no, Rome! What did you do!" Chyna cried as she shook her brother.

"It's alright, Chy. I love you, baby girl," Rome said before he closed his eyes.

At that point, everything else was a blur. The next thing she knew, she was being put into an ambulance, and Maddox was calling her name over and over.

The paramedics pulled Chyna's stretcher out of the ambulance and rushed her through the emergency room with Rome right behind her. She had no idea who was out to get her, but somebody was. It was no coincidence that the first day she came outside, she got shot at. The person didn't even start shooting until they were close to where she was, and now her brother was hurt because of her. If it was the last thing, she did, she was going to find out who was responsible for trying to ruin her life. She just prayed that Rome was alright.

"Miss, we need you to calm down. We need to see where your injuries are. There's a lot of blood on you," the doctor said as he cut Chyna's shirt open and examined her body.

"I'm fine, I need to check on my brother."

"You're a very lucky, young lady. It looks like the bullet went straight through your upper arm. I see an entrance and exit wound. We'll still have to do an x-ray to make sure nothing is broken. After that, we can give you some antibiotics, pain medication, and a tetanus shot. Then, we'll stitch up, and you should be able to go."

"Alright," Chyna replied.

After three hours of getting treatment and examined, Chyna was discharged. She went straight to the waiting room where her family was, so that she could get an update on her brother.

"Oh my, God, Chyna. I'm so glad that you're alright," Mrs. Black cried as she pulled Chyna into her.

"Ouch, Ma. I'm fine. Did you bring me some clothes?"

"Yeah, I did, I'm sorry. Are you alright?"

"I'll be fine, I was only hit in the shoulder. It was an in and out wound. How is Rome doing?"

"He's still in surgery, baby. They haven't told us much yet. We just know he took two bullets. One was in his chest, and the other one in his side."

Chyna put on the shirt that her mother gave her. She didn't worry about changing her pants yet because she was starting to feel lightheaded.

"Alright, I need to step outside to get some air," said Chyna.

"I'll go with you," offered Maddox.

Maddox and Chyna stepped outside, and Yakea came running their way.

"Oh my, God, Chyna! Are you alright?" asked Yakea.

"I'm good, Kea, why are you running though?"

"Girl, I just got out of my car and as I was walking this way when I saw the nigga that I was telling you about. The thing is I didn't tell you this, but I'm pregnant by him, and he's here with his wife. Do you think I should confront them or not?"

"Just be cool for a minute, Kea. I'm just trying to make sure everything is good with my brother. I can't deal with anymore drama, right now," said Chyna.

"Okay, just for you, I'll be cool but what should I do? It looks like they're coming this way."

Chyna looked in the same direction as Kea to see who she

was looking at. There were a few people heading that way to the main entrance, including Nathan and Chloe.

Which one," was the last thing Chyna got out before the dizziness had taken over. She felt Maddox catch her before she hit the ground, but after that, everything went black.

❧

"ALRIGHT, I THINK THAT'S ENOUGH FOR TODAY. I'M TIRED AND I'm not ready to relieve one of the most emotional days of my life yet," Chyna stated as she stopped talking about her life and stood from the couch. She needed time to gain her composure.

"What? Are you serious? We were just doing so good. You can't just stop there; I need to know what happened. Who is Kea's baby father? Did Rome survive that day? What ended up happening to your court case? Most importantly, how did you choose who you were going to have your happily ever after with?" questioned Dr. Taylor.

Chyna smiled at the therapist's reactions. That was one of the main reasons she wasn't ready to open up yet because she knew once she started, she would want to know everything. At that point, Chyna could've said she was no longer going to pay her, and she still would have continued to listen to her life story.

"I'm sorry, I'll tell you what. How about we pick up where we left off at in a few weeks, and I promise to answer all of your questions. I won't leave anything unanswered. Do we have a deal?" Chyna asked.

"Yeah, I understand. Just make sure you hold up your end of the deal when I come back, Chyna. We don't need you to take any steps back. You did so well opening up to me, today. I'm proud of you for the big step you've taken."

"Don't worry, I will," Chyna assured her.

To Be Continued....

AUTHOR NOTES

Whew, it's been so long since I've written a note to my readers that I don't even know where to begin. I guess, first, I would like to say thank you, thank you, thank you for the continuous support. For those of you that don't know, I have been writing since 2013. It has been quite a journey. Without the support of you all, I wouldn't have lasted this long. I love to tell the story of how I first started because someone else may be experiencing the same thing and not even know what to do.

The story line of my first book started because one night, I was sitting down in the house bored and an idea came to me out of nowhere, but I ignored it. The next day while I was at work, the same idea came back, but this time, it came it came as a vision in my mind. I literally saw the entire scene play out in my head and was blown away. Like, what the hell is wrong with me, lol. Fast forward a couple of days, and it was still there, so I pulled out a pen and paper to get the thoughts out of my head. By the time I looked up, I had 2,000 words and so forth and so on until I ended with 30,000 and then 40,000. Even still, I had all type of doubts and had no idea what I wanted to do with the book. In my mind, I was like who would want to read my work? Nobody even knows who I am. I had a couple of people that I were close to in the industry at the time, and they encouraged me along the way. The best advice I had got from one of them was, "The only way that you can truly fail is if you never try."

I say all of this to say, if an idea or thought comes to you, stop ignoring it and use it to your advantage. You never know; that might just be the next classic. It might even be just what someone needed to heal their heart. You should never give up because dreams don't come true unless you work. Anything is possible if you push yourself hard enough and believe in yourself. I love connecting with my readers as well as hearing your thoughts on my work.

Follow me on Facebook: Author Kevina Hopkins or Kevina
Bawsette Hopkins
Twitter: Vina2006
Instagram: caramel_skin_27
Stay up to date with upcoming sneak peeks and contests by
joining my mailing list. Text your email address to keyword
KEVINAHOPKINS at 22828

CONTEST
For your chance to win a Kindle join my mailing list and
screenshot your proof of purchase. Send it to
uniquepenngiveaways@gmail.com

CPSIA information can be obtained
at www.ICGtesting.com
Printed in the USA
LVHW041946061120
670968LV00003B/481